PUFFIN BOOKS

WHAT A WEEK TO PLAY IT COOL

'Holly, just go and get on with homework or some-thing, will you? I'm not feeling too hot and I don't need all this.'

'Oh, don't you?' shouted Holly. 'And I don't need you to tell me how to spend my life! And what's more, I'm not going to let you. I'm going to that concert, Dad, whether you like it or not.'

Easy Reading (ER)

What a Week to Play it Cool

Rosie Rushton

PUFFIN BOOKS

For the cool kids of
Montsaye School, Rothwell

PUFFIN BOOKS

Published by the Penguin Group
Penguin Books Ltd, 27 Wrights Lane, London W8 5TZ, England
Penguin Putnam Inc., 375 Hudson Street, New York, New York 10014, USA
Penguin Books Australia Ltd, Ringwood, Victoria, Australia
Penguin Books Canada Ltd, 10 Alcorn Avenue, Toronto, Ontario, Canada M4V 3B2
Penguin Books (NZ) Ltd, Private Bag 102902, NSMC, Auckland, New Zealand

On the World Wide Web at: www.penguin.com

Penguin Books Ltd, Registered Offices: Harmondsworth, Middlesex, England

First published 1999
3 5 7 9 10 8 6 4 2

Set in 12/14pt Monotype Baskerville by
Rowland Phototypesetting Ltd, Bury St Edmunds, Suffolk
Made and printed in England by Clays Ltd, St Ives plc

British Library Cataloguing in Publication Data
A CIP catalogue record for this book is available from the British Library

ISBN 0–141–30491–X

MONDAY

'I love you, I love you, I love you!' Holly Vine leaned forward and planted a long, lingering kiss on Paul's lips.

Paul grinned down at her from the wall. The poster had cost her an absolute fortune, but it had been worth every penny. Admittedly, it was a bit fuzzy round the edges – Paul's hair appeared to be suffering from static electricity and his left ear was blurry – but the man in the photographic shop said that was what happened when people wanted to turn one rather second-rate negative into a one-metre-square poster.

'You'd do better having a nice little picture in a frame, me duck,' he had advised her, but then he was forty if he was a day and had probably never been in love in his life. Holly had plenty of small

1

photographs of Paul – one in her school bag, one slipped into her key fob, another stuck on her homework diary – but this was like having him in her bedroom with her. And since, she thought, stroking his chin with her forefinger, she didn't see him in the flesh nearly often enough, this was the next best thing.

She blew him a final kiss and pulled open her underwear drawer, searching for her new mega-padded, supreme uplift, squeeze-it-all-together bra. That was something else that had made a huge hole in her monthly allowance, but the lady in the shop said you only got what you paid for, and Holly reckoned fifteen pounds was a small price to pay if it would make her look halfway normal. She was getting really worried about what was happening to her, or rather, what wasn't happening. All her friends were growing up normally and at the right speed and she wasn't. She still had lopsided boobs and her body didn't go in and out like Cleo's or Jade's, it just went straight up and down. But what was far worse, she thought, squirting herself with a large amount of *It Girl* body mist, was that she couldn't be sure that Paul really, really loved her.

She had done the *'Does He Pass The True Love Test?'* quiz in *Heaven Sent* magazine and it had confirmed her innermost fears. Paul had fallen into the 'Mostly B's' category, which meant that he was a Shy Boy; a guy afraid of admitting his true feelings. Of course, this explained why Paul was being off with her. Well, not off exactly, but certainly not as on as she would like. He was friendly enough; in fact, he was always asking her out – but all he ever wanted to do was play tennis or badminton, or go roller skating or bowling. Even at the cinema he seemed more interested in the film than in long, lingering looks or kisses that went on forever. It all made Holly feel very inadequate.

But, she thought, pulling on her school sweater and ramming her feet into her boots, from now on, things were going to change. She was going to change her tactics completely: stop being as meek and mild as she had been since that awful row, when she had accused Paul of two-timing her and made herself look a total idiot, and make it quite clear to him that he was the only one for her.

'Once he knows that you really care, he'll come out of his shell,' her best friend Tansy had assured her knowledgeably. 'That type always do.'

Holly hoped very much that she was right. She'd dreamed yet again of floating along a palm-fringed beach, her arm linked through Paul's, her white wedding dress billowing out, blown by the tropical breeze while Paul whispered 'I love you, my darling' in her left ear. She knew the wedding was a long way off, but right now she was determined to get to the 'I love you' bit, whatever it took. And today was when the campaign would begin in earnest.

That was why she was up and dressed so early. On Mondays, Paul caught the early bus to do circuit training at his school, Bishop Agnew College, and she had to catch him before he left. She opened the top drawer of her dressing table and took out the neatly wrapped little package. She had it all planned: she would meet him at the bus stop, really casual and laid back. Then she would slip the wicked present into his pocket, say something cool but with suitably seductive overtones and then walk on.

She was just picturing the look of desire that would undoubtedly spread over Paul's gorgeous face, when her parents' bedroom door slammed so violently that the lampshade above Holly's head shook.

'Have you taken leave of your senses? How could you contemplate doing something so completely ridiculous?'

Her mother's voice grew more shrill with every word.

'Oh well, that's typical of you, isn't it?' Holly's father interjected. 'Just because I make a perfectly rational suggestion . . .'

'Rational? Insane, more like!' Holly could hear her mother thudding downstairs.

'Now, just you hang on a moment – Angela!'

More stomping, a few muffled expletives, and then the kitchen door slammed.

Holly sighed and squirted Shine Serum into

the palm of her hand. It was, she thought, running her fingers through her nutmeg-brown hair, quite remarkable that parents who went totally ballistic if they caught her playing indie music at anything above a low murmur, thought nothing of disturbing the peace like a pair of football hooligans the moment they had even a minor disagreement. And they had been having those quite a lot lately.

They never used to be like that. Oh, her parents had always been a problem, of course, but Holly had got used to her mother making a public spectacle of herself in the name of so-called good causes, and she had even learned to tolerate her father's extraordinary obsession with dressing up as a Roundhead and running amok with a pikestaff whenever he got the chance. But, at least until now, they had just ignored one another and got on with their own sad lives, which meant she could get on with hers. Her father's latest burst of stupidity threatened to put a stop to all that.

It was only the week before that a gobsmacked Holly had witnessed a humdinger of a row between her warring parents.

'What do you mean, we'll take in a lodger?' her mother had exploded. 'What on earth would we want to do that for?'

'This house costs a fortune to keep up,' he had replied briskly. 'The central heating boiler needs replacing, there are slates missing from the roof, the window frames are rotting . . .'

'So let's sell up and move to a nice modern house,' Holly's mother had chipped in hopefully.

'Don't be so ridiculous!' her father had retorted. 'There have been Vines living at The Cedars for –'

'Over a hundred years,' her mother had finished wearily. 'I know. I just thought maybe we could set a new trend.'

Holly's father hadn't deigned to reply, but had continued scribbling figures on the back of an envelope, running his fingers through his grey hair and frowning anxiously.

'No,' he had said decisively. 'Paying guests – that's the answer. We'll turn Richard's old room into a bedsit and if that works, we can do the same with Tom's.'

Of course, Holly's mother had protested loudly, saying that she didn't have any time to go running round after lodgers, what with her work at the Day Centre, and Meals on Wheels, and her father had thumped the table and said that if she could put her very obvious organizational skills to full-time employment instead of devoting every day to lost causes, they might not have to worry about money quite so much. And then Holly's mum had gone red in the face and said that most men would be proud to have a wife with a social conscience, and her dad had sniffed and said that most men might be able to afford one but *he couldn't*.

'Besides,' Holly had interjected, realizing that

someone had to add a note of sanity to the argument, 'we don't want strangers living in the house. They'd get in the way.'

'Exactly,' her mother had agreed, nodding gratefully, 'and you never know what sort of person you would get.'

'Oh, don't you worry about all that!' her father had said airily. 'I think I've found the very chap already.'

'You what?'

Holly's mother had spat the words through gritted teeth.

'He's called José Cavellero,' said Rupert.

'Ho-say who?' interjected Holly.

'He's from Madrid University. The friend of my old professor's cousin's wife. Or was it his wife's cousin?'

He had caught sight of Mrs Vine's tight-lipped expression.

'But no matter,' he had concluded hastily, 'it will probably come to nothing.'

Since then, Holly had thought it had all blown over, but judging by the racket coming from behind the closed kitchen door, it sounded very much as if it had all suddenly come to something after all.

Holly grabbed her school bag and headed downstairs.

'I cannot believe you just said that!' Angela Vine shouted as Holly pushed open the kitchen door.

'Well, you had better believe it, because I'm not going to change my mind!'

'Oh, aren't you? Well, let me tell you here and now . . .'

'Will you two shut up!' Holly slammed her bag down on the floor, yanked open the refrigerator door and eyed the worryingly empty shelves. 'Mum, there's no milk.'

'Milk? Milk? Never mind milk!' her mother stormed. 'Have you heard your father's latest piece of nonsense?'

'The lodger? This Hozay guy?' Holly decided against the idea of cereal and grabbed the last remaining yoghurt.

'Oh my goodness! The lodger!' Her father stared at her open-mouthed.

'Well, that's what all this yelling is about, isn't it?' demanded Holly, ripping the top off her yoghurt pot. 'We are going to have to put up with some stuffy –'

'No, no, it's worse than that!' interjected her mother, turning on the tap and filling the kettle. 'Although now, of course, I realize why he is so keen to take in strangers off the street. It's just his way of funding his own selfish desires!'

'Mum, what are you on about?' Holly asked wearily.

'Your dear father is only intending to resign – today – just like that! He's going to throw in a perfectly good job!'

'What?' Holly stared at her father open-mouthed. 'Why on earth do you want to do that?'

For as long as she could remember, her dad had been lecturing at the university, spouting about history on deadly dull late-night radio programmes and writing boring books about army generals who had been dead for hundreds of years. It was dead uncool, but it kept him out of the way.

'To preserve my sanity,' he replied. 'Tell me, what day is it today?'

'I'll tell you why he's doing it,' babbled her mother, ignoring him totally. 'He is planning to spend the rest of his life running some half-baked little museum in the middle of nowhere!'

'A museum?' Holly eyed her paternal parent with amazement. 'Dad, are you crazy?'

'Not at all,' he murmured. 'Er, what's today?'

'Monday,' said Holly, spooning yoghurt into her mouth. 'And will you please explain to me what is going on?'

'It's simple,' said her father decisively. 'I'm to be the new curator of The Battlefield Museum at Little Kidlington. Lovely place. Been allowed to run down a bit but I have scores of ideas and with a bit of Lottery money and some –'

'But why, Dad?'

'Why? In a word, I'm tired of the rat race of the university, the lack of funding, tired of dancing to everyone else's tune. Because I'm nearly sixty years old and for once in my life I want to do something just for me. Before it's too late.'

He paused, frowning.

'Monday the what?'

Holly's mother sighed.

'Monday the fifth,' she said impatiently. 'Why?'

'The fifth,' repeated Holly's father. 'I am sure something was meant to be happening on the fifth.'

'You've probably got yet another meeting about the Town Pageant,' said his wife, throwing tea bags into the pot.

'Ah, the Pageant!' exclaimed Rupert, a look of relief spreading over his face. 'That must be what I was thinking of. Looking forward to Saturday, are you, Holly?'

Holly shrugged. She was hardly going to admit to being excited about anything with which her father was remotely connected – and besides, although it was cool being on the School Float Committee, it would mean another whole Saturday apart from Paul. It was OK for her mates, whose boyfriends all went to West Green Upper with them; but Paul would be on the Bishop Agnew float and they might not even be in the same part of the procession. She just had to find a way of making sure that once the judging was over, they spent the rest of the day together.

'It'll be OK,' she said, peering into the bread bin. 'MUM! There isn't any bread either. You'll have to go shopping. Tansy's staying the night – we'll starve at this rate!'

'Come to think of it,' added Mrs Vine, spinning round to face her husband, 'you could do the supermarket shop when you've finished resigning. Now there's a good idea!'

'Me?' Rupert look astounded. 'Well, of course I would but actually, I'm not feeling too hot. I think I pulled a muscle at the battle rehearsal last week and –'

'You'll have to come up with a better excuse than that!' retorted his wife. 'I wasn't born yesterday!'

At that moment, the carriage clock in the adjoining sitting room chimed the half hour.

'I've got to dash,' cried Holly, realizing that in all the furore she had forgotten the time. 'I'll see you tonight.'

She pecked her mother on the cheek and snatched her jacket off the back of the chair.

'Holly, you can't go yet! You haven't eaten.'

'Whose fault's that?' called Holly from the hall. 'Besides, Paul . . .'

The moment the word was out of her mouth she regretted it.

'Oh, Holly, really!' her mother protested, peering into the back of the fridge. 'You can see Paul any time. A good breakfast is far more important than chasing after boys. I've found some bacon.'

'Your mother's right,' agreed her father. 'In fact, research has shown –'

'Bye!' Holly ignored her father's protests about missed meals leading to falling grades and slammed the front door behind her. She couldn't believe that she would ever be old enough to think that a couple of rashers of bacon mattered more than love and romance. Besides, she had read that people in love got fewer colds than those on the shelf, so who needed protein?

It was as she reached the end of their gravel drive, turning up her collar against the steady drizzle, that she saw the Bishop Agnew College bus pulling up at the stop on the corner. Among the crowd of boys jostling their way through the doors, she caught a glimpse of Paul's fair head.

'Hi, Paul! Paul, wait!' she called, breaking into a run.

He couldn't hear her. She forced her legs to run faster, her school bag bouncing on her shoulder and her hand gripping the parcel in her pocket.

'Paul!'

A stockily built guy spotted her and nudged Paul. He turned, gave her a casual wave and clambered on board the bus. Holly had just reached the stop when the bus doors closed.

'Paul!' she called, tapping on the window. 'Paul!'

He glanced up as he pushed his way down the gangway, his cheeks turning an endearing shade of pink.

'I'll catch you tonight, OK?' she shouted. 'I've got something for you.'

'Way-hay! Roll on tonight, Paul!'

'You're on to a winner there, Paul mate!'

Holly could see his friends pointing at her and slapping Paul on the shoulders.

'So that's the famous girlfriend, is it?' shouted the stocky guy. 'Well, aren't you going to blow her a kiss, lover boy?'

Paul turned and gave her a weak smile as the bus pulled away. At any other time she might have been disappointed by his reticence, but right now her heart was soaring. The famous girlfriend, that was what the guy had said. Paul had obviously been so proud of her that he had told all his mates how he felt! He clearly *did care about her* – if only she could get him to tell her so!

It didn't matter that she had missed him this morning; it didn't matter that she hadn't been able to give him her present yet. She was going to work out a plan that meant getting him to herself this weekend.

The sooner she managed to do that, the better it would be for both of them.

7.50 a.m. 53 Lime Avenue, Oak Hill, Dunchester. Tired of playing Florence Nightingale

'Are you going to get up or not?' Jade Williams shook the groaning heap under the red and white striped duvet for the fifth time that morning.

'Go away!' Her cousin opened one eye and scowled at her. 'Can't you see I'm dying?'

'You do look a weird colour,' admitted Jade, peering closely at Allegra. 'I'll get Paula.'

'No! Don't!' At the mention of her mother's name, Allegra swung her long legs out of the bed and sat up.

'Why not?'

'She'll only fuss and . . . oh, my head!'

'Have a glass of water, that might help,' volunteered Jade, zipping up her school skirt. 'And I'll bring you up a cup of tea.'

'I don't want a glass of water!' snapped Allegra, struggling to her feet. 'I don't want a cup of tea! I just want to be left in peace, OK? Can't you stop going on and on?'

'Oh, please yourself!' Jade grabbed her sweater from the back of her chair and strode over to the door. 'And next time you want someone to hold your hand while you throw up, don't look at me!'

She slammed the bedroom door, deliberately ignoring Allegra's wail of protest, and stomped down the stairs. It was bad enough having to share a bedroom with Allegra when she was in what passed for one of her good moods; sleeping two metres away from her when she was groaning and thrashing about and threatening to expire at any moment was more than the human frame could stand. Ever since Jade had moved in with her aunt's family after the death of her parents, her uncle had been promising faithfully to get a move on with converting the attic into a bedroom for her; sadly his time-management skills were not on a par with his ability as a banker, and apart from purchasing a tin of white emulsion and a new set of screwdrivers, not a lot had been achieved.

As she reached the bottom of the stairs she almost fell over Joshua, her sixteen-year-old dweeb of a cousin, who was crawling on his hands and knees along the hall floor.

'What are you doing?' she demanded.

'I've lost Josephine,' he said forlornly.

'Excuse me?'

'My praying mantis,' he explained. 'You haven't seen her, have you?'

'If I had,' replied Jade curtly, 'you'd have heard about it.'

Sad or what? thought Jade. Sixteen years old and the only female he is passionate about is an insect. She pushed open the kitchen door and headed straight for the fridge. Her aunt, dressed in scarlet leggings and a baggy sweater across which trotted three felt ducks, was scrambling eggs and singing along with Radio Two so loudly that she didn't hear the door open. Jade grabbed a carton of orange juice, slumped down on a chair and stretched her legs out under the kitchen table – and promptly leaped up again at the sound of an angry yelp.

'Helen,' she asked her eight-year-old cousin patiently, 'why are you under the table?'

'It's an air-raid shelter,' replied Helen, 'and I'm about to give birth.'

'Oh, Jade, there you are!' Paula cried. 'Don't worry, they're doing the Blitz in history, and she is taking it all very seriously. Did you sleep well, darling?

'Not really,' sighed Jade. 'Allegra spent the night preparing to die.'

'She did *what*?'

Paula slammed the Off button of the radio and looked alarmed.

Jade sighed.

'First she felt sick, then she said her head hurt, then she wanted more covers on and then she wanted the window open. And when she did go to sleep, she snored. It wasn't very peaceful.'

'Oh, poor child!' Paula thrust the wooden spoon into Jade's hands. 'You dish up the eggs – I must go to her.'

She was pulling off her apron when the door opened and Allegra shuffled in, wrapped in her purple towelling bathrobe.

'Allegra darling!' Paula grabbed her hand. 'Jade says you're poorly.'

Allegra gave a wan smile, tiredly flicked her hair over her shoulder and sank into the nearest vacant chair, passing a weary hand over her brow.

'I'll be all right,' she said in the tones of one who

deserves a medal for courage in the face of extreme adversity. 'It's nothing much.'

It was clear, thought Jade, tipping scrambled eggs on to plates, that Allegra's years at the local stage school enabled her to play the tragic heroine with great success.

'I don't want to make a fuss,' her cousin continued, fiddling with the corner of the tablecloth.

'You wanted to all last night!' burst out Jade, slamming plates on the table.

Her aunt glared at her and put a hand on Allegra's forehead.

'Did you eat something odd at Hugo's house last night?' she asked anxiously. 'I have to say, Mrs Timbrell does seem to be less than meticulous on the hygiene front.'

'Oh, Mum, don't start that again!' Allegra snapped out of pathetic mode. 'I know you've got it in for Hugo . . .'

'Not at all, dear, I just think –'

There was a groan from under the table.

'What's that?' Allegra asked.

'Helen's in labour,' said Jade wryly, forking the last morsel of egg into her mouth. 'Don't ask.'

'Now can you eat something, darling?' fluttered Paula. 'And perhaps you should have some paracetamol. Or would milk of magnesia be best?'

'Oh, for heaven's sake, Mum!' retorted Allegra. 'I'll just go back to bed and sleep it off.'

Paula ran her fingers through her hair.

'This couldn't have happened at a worse time,' she sighed. 'You've got the auditions for *Flying High* on Thursday.'

'It's no big deal,' muttered Allegra.

'But if you miss it . . .'

'I won't!' she retorted. 'I'll be better by then. I just need a day off, that's all.'

'But is that a good idea, darling? I mean, if you are off school today, you'll miss the dance rehearsal and that will give Tamsin and Candice an advantage. And I know how much getting a part in this show means to you.'

For once, Allegra didn't come back with a clever remark. She merely dropped her eyes and began fiddling with the belt of her bathrobe.

'Just think,' continued Paula, 'my daughter, playing in a West End musical! I am so proud of you!'

'Mum, I haven't been chosen yet and besides –'

'I know, I know, but Mrs Armstrong says you're a natural. So we have to make sure you're fit for the auditions. You have been practising that song, haven't you, angel?'

'Yes,' said Allegra shortly. 'Look, it's OK, Mum, I'm feeling better by the minute.'

'Really?' Paula's face brightened instantly.

'Really,' said Allegra. 'I'll go up and get dressed.'

'Well, darling, if you are quite sure . . .' Paula's

enquiries were interrupted by the shrilling of the front door bell.

'Oh no!' Allegra pulled her bathrobe more tightly round her and wrenched open the kitchen door. 'That'll be Hugo – I'd forgotten that he said he'd call for me. Don't open the door till I've gone upstairs. And don't say a word about me being sick. Promise?'

'Why?' Her mother looked puzzled.

'Just don't, OK? Promise me?'

Paula shrugged.

'Don't worry,' interrupted Jade, peering down the hall to the glass-panelled front door. 'It's not Hugo – it's Scott.'

Allegra, looking visibly relieved, turned and headed upstairs.

'I've just given birth to quads,' Helen announced, crawling out from under the table as Jade squeezed past her. 'And our house has been bombed and we are homeless and desiccated.'

'Destitute,' corrected her mother.

'I've found her!' Josh rushed past Jade, his hands cupped against his chest. 'She's in shock! Out of the way, quickly!'

Jade sighed deeply, shook her head in despair and opened the front door.

'Scott,' she said pleadingly before he could open his mouth. 'Will you do something for me?'

'Of course,' he said, looking puzzled. 'What?'

'Take me away from all this. Like now.'

Monday

'Hey, Andy! Where are you? It's me!'

Tansy Meadows lifted the letter box of 11 Fishponds Road and called again.

'Andy, get a move on – we'll be late!'

What's more, she thought, anxiously patting her freshly styled hair in place, if she spent much longer on his doorstep in this force-eight gale, the stunning effect of her new Volumizing Uplift Perm with Added Sheen would be totally lost. She reckoned that her new hairstyle gave her an air of subtle sophistication, which it jolly well should consider-ing how much it had cost her. Ever since Ella Hankinson had told her that she looked like a dying dandelion, Tansy had been determined to do something about her wispy, flyaway hair. It was, she had always considered, one of Nature's gross injustices that instead of inheriting her mother's great mass of golden, curly hair, she had been lum-bered with the nondescript sandy-coloured tresses that were obviously a hand-me-down from her father's genes. When she was younger, she had yearned to look like the dad she had never known, but imagined to be handsome and successful; now that she knew the truth about him she resented every characteristic that might have come from him.

A gust of wind swirled some stray leaves round her feet and ruffled her feather fringe as she

20

punched the doorbell once more. Within seconds, the door swung open and Andy appeared, tight-lipped and quite obviously not at peace with the world.

'Just cool it, can't you?' he shouted, pushing his spectacles up on the bridge of his nose. 'Stop making such a racket!'

'Sorr-ee!' Tansy's eyebrows shot upwards. 'What's with you this morning?'

'Oh, just come in and shut up!' Andy waved her impatiently into the hall and slammed the front door.

'Andy, what on earth is the matter?'

'Ssshhh!' Andy laid his finger to his lips and jerked his head towards his father's study. 'Dad's on the phone.'

From behind the closed door, Tansy could hear the low murmur of a conversation in progress:

'Look, I just can't get my head round this. I don't know what to think!'

She recognized the gravelly tones of Andy's father.

'So are you telling me . . . ?'

His voice dropped and Andy moved closer to the door, screwing up his face as he strained to catch the next phrase.

'What's going on?' Tansy ventured to enquire. 'What's the big deal?'

'BE QUIET! I'm trying to listen.'

'I can't talk now. Yes, yes, I'll call you later. Bye!'

21

There was a click as the handset was replaced and Andy wheeled round to face Tansy.

'What did you have to keep burbling on for?' he demanded, red in the face. 'Now I don't know whether it was . . .' His voice faltered.

'Whether it was what?' asked Tansy shortly, none too pleased at being yelled at first thing on a Monday morning.

At that moment the study door opened and Mr Richards emerged, muttering under his breath. As he spotted Andy and Tansy, the frown on his broad brow deepened.

'Andy, what the blazes are you doing hanging about here?' he demanded, glancing irritably at his watch. 'It's gone eight o'clock!'

'We were just off, Mr Richards,' intervened Tansy hastily. 'Ready, Andy?'

Andy swallowed and bent down to tie his flapping trainer laces.

'Who was that on the phone?' he asked, his voice coming out as a strangled squeak.

'What?' His father suddenly found a speck of dirt under his thumbnail to be of extraordinary interest. 'Oh, er – a colleague from the office. With a problem.'

Andy shot him a penetrating glance.

'What colleague?'

'Andy, it's none of your business!' snapped his father. 'Now will you please get going? And where's Ricky?'

'Gone,' said Andy, shrugging his arms into his jacket.

'You let him go on his own? Andy, how could you? I rely on you to keep an eye on him.'

'Dad, he's ten, for heaven's sake,' retorted Andy. 'And he only has to go two hundred yards. He's got to grow up some time.'

His father sighed.

'I know, I know,' he said. 'It's just that now that everything is down to me . . .'

He shook himself.

'Anyway, off you go – and have a good day.'

'Yeah,' mumbled Andy in tones that suggested that he thought it highly unlikely that the day would be anything other than totally dire.

As they walked down the path and into the street, Tansy waited for Andy to slip his hand into hers, to tell her how cool she looked or to crack one of his weird alien-type jokes. But he merely shoved his hands into his pockets and stomped along the pavement, kicking the odd stray can into the gutter with vicious fury.

'Andy, what's wrong?' she demanded after five minutes of total silence.

'Nothing,' muttered Andy

'Oh right!' retorted Tansy sarcastically as they turned the corner into Weston Way. 'You look as if you could commit murder, you haven't opened your mouth since we left and you say nothing's wrong. So what was with the great drama over your dad speaking to some colleague on the phone?'

Andy stopped and hitched his school bag higher on to his shoulder.

'I don't reckon it was anyone from his office,' he blurted out. 'I'm almost sure it was . . .'

He scuffed the toe of his shoe against the kerb.

'Yes?' Tansy urged.

'I think it was my mum.'

'Your *mum*?' Tansy gasped. 'Surely not?'

Andy's mother had walked out on her family several months before, and apart from getting a whole load of postcards from different towns and cities in England and Scotland, and parcels through the post on birthdays, the family hadn't heard from her since.

'And why not?' retorted Andy with a catch in his voice. 'Why shouldn't she want to phone us?'

Tansy touched his arm as they started walking again.

'I didn't mean it like that,' she said hastily. 'But surely, if it *had* been your mum, your dad would have told you. I mean, he'd be over the moon at hearing from her after so long.'

Andy shrugged and chewed on his thumbnail.

'I don't know,' he said. 'All I know is that I heard Dad say "Val!", you know, all surprised like, when he picked up the phone.'

Tansy frowned.

'But if it had been her, she would have asked to speak to you, wouldn't she?'

'I suppose so,' sighed Andy, as they reached the school gates. 'I guess I was just imagining things.'

Tansy tried desperately to think of something to take his mind off his troubles.

'Hey,' she said brightly, 'about Saturday. Are you going?'

Andy frowned.

'To the Pageant? We have to, don't we? I mean, it's our float and even if we're not on it, we have to wander about with collecting buckets and stuff.'

'No, silly, I mean afterwards,' said Tansy. 'To this.'

She pulled a crumpled advertisement from her jacket pocket and thrust it into his hands.

Andy squinted through his spectacles and scanned the sheet.

'Wow!' he gasped. 'Shiny Vinyl! That would be so cool!'

He sighed and thrust the paper back in her hand.

'Not that I've got fifteen pounds to spare,' he said.

'Couldn't you ask your dad?' suggested Tansy hopefully. 'I mean, tell him it's for charity and all that and . . .'

Andy looked doubtful.

'I could try,' he said, pushing open the double doors to the main building. 'I don't hold out much hope though. He's had to work shorter hours since Mum went off . . .'

His voice trailed off.

'I'm really sorry about your mum and everything,' Tansy said. 'I know what it's like – well, sort of. I mean, when I was trying to find out about my real dad, I couldn't think about anything else and it was awful when my mum tried to fob me off all the time.'

Andy nodded.

'So you'll just have to confront him,' Tansy declared.

'What?' Andy looked as if confronting his father was only marginally less alarming than taking on a pack of marauding hyenas.

'Ask him straight. Say you heard him using your mother's name on the phone and that you are fourteen and a half years old and have a right to know what is going on.'

Andy bit his lip.

'I suppose I could, couldn't I?' he ventured.

Tansy nodded encouragingly.

'You're not a child,' she said. 'He mustn't treat you like one. Parents are very bad at learning that lesson.'

'You're right!' Andy said. 'I'll do it tonight.'

He paused.

'I don't suppose you fancy coming over after school? Moral support and all that.'

Tansy sighed.

'I can't – I'm sleeping over at Holly's. My mother's gone to some horticultural society meeting in Torquay. Besides,' she added firmly, 'this is between you and your dad.'

'I guess,' sighed Andy. 'And after all, he wouldn't lie to his own son, would he?'

It occurred to Tansy that he seemed to be having great difficulty convincing himself that that was true.

8.30 a.m. Pretending this is not happening
If I just keep walking, thought Cleo Greenway, I can pretend that this isn't happening. Just look straight ahead and pray that no one has noticed.

'Hey, Cleo! Wait!'

Holly bounded up the hill behind her and grabbed her arm.

'Look, Cleo! There's your mum! On the side of that bus!'

Cleo shuddered.

'Don't remind me,' she groaned, averting her eyes as the bus thundered past.

Ever since her mother had been selected as the mature model for Fittinix, the Gasp-Free Control Pant, Cleo had been subjected to one cringe-making experience after another. She would be watching TV with Trig, only to have some romantic film interrupted by the sight of her mother's bottom hanging out of a balloon while she told the entire universe that Fittinix gave middle-aged tummies man appeal. Only last week she had been poring over a fashion magazine with Jade, only to turn a page and see her own mother, who was old enough to know better, pouting from a full colour photograph with the caption 'Diana Greenway, Actress and Model, proves that age is no barrier to looking sexy'. And now there she was, stuck on the side of a bus. Not just any bus. The school bus.

'You're so lucky to have a glamorous, laid-back kind of mother,' sighed Holly as they crossed the road towards school. 'Mine's all tweed skirts and good works – it's very boring.'

'I think,' said Cleo, casting one last, reluctant look at the offending bus, 'I'd settle for boring any day.'

They were about to turn into the school gates when Holly stopped dead and grabbed Cleo's arm again.

'Look!' she said, pointing to the nearby lamp post on which was tied a cardboard poster. 'Hot Totty! And Shiny Vinyl!' She dragged Cleo over to the notice. 'See? Saturday night – at The Bowl!'

'Nice,' murmured Cleo.

'Nice? Nice?' Holly stared at her. 'It's more than nice – it's perfect! It'll be so brilliant – all those bands, and the dancing and smooching and . . .'

'Oh, sure!' taunted Cleo. 'As if! My mother would go ballistic if she thought I was going some-where like that. Wouldn't yours?'

'Probably,' said Holly. 'But I'm going anyway. It could be the answer to all my dreams.'

8.50 a.m. In the locker room

'Hey, Tansy, you'll never guess what!'

'What?'

'There's this amazing concert at The Bowl on Saturday with . . .'

'Yes, I know. Rock-It. I'd die to go,' said Tansy.

'Well, I am going!' enthused Holly.

'You are?'

'Yes,' said Holly smugly. 'With Paul.'

Tansy's eyes widened.

'So you've sorted things – what happened? What did he say? Has he got the tickets already?'

Holly looked awkward.

'Well, not exactly. I mean, I haven't asked him yet. I only saw the poster on the way to school.'

'Holly!'

'OK, OK,' replied Holly. 'I'm going to ask him tonight, when I take his present round.'

She sighed and closed her eyes dreamily.

'Just think,' she murmured, 'six whole hours of smooching with Paul.'

'He hasn't said yes yet,' Tansy reminded her.

'He will,' said Holly. 'He has to. Because if he doesn't, I shall die.'

Monday

'Well now, boys and girls, here we all are at the beginning of another week!' Mr Boardman, the headmaster, beamed benignly round the room. 'And what a week!'

A few bottoms shuffled on the floor in preparation for what everyone expected to be a long speech.

'I don't need to remind you that Wednesday is Open Day . . .'

A low groan rippled round the room as he waffled on about clean shirts and neatly knotted ties and being polite to visitors and not whistling in the corridors.

'. . . And then, of course, on Saturday we have the Town Pageant.'

He clasped his hands to his chest ecstatically.

'Our Marching Band will be taking part, and Years Eight and Nine are entering a float, about which, in a moment, Holly Vine will have a few words . . .'

'I will?' Holly looked at Tansy in alarm.

'About choosing who's going on the float,' Tansy reminded her.

'Oh, that,' said Holly and returned to picking the polish off her thumbnail.

'And today, one of our greatest achievements yet,' the head continued. 'The third round of the Inter Schools Rugby Competition, here at West

Green Upper. Never before has a local state school got this far in the competition and I want you all to turn out to cheer on our first team.'

'Boring!' Tansy muttered in Holly's ear.

Mr Boardman cleared his throat and eyed them sternly.

'For those of you who don't follow rugby, our team will be playing against Bishop Agnew College.'

Holly gasped.

'You know what that means?' she whispered.

Tansy grinned.

'Paul!' they whispered in unison.

9.15 a.m. With her mind on other things

'. . . So everyone who wants to be on Paul – I mean, on the float must put their names in the bucket in the Art Room by lunchtime,' announced Holly from the platform. 'Then Mr Boardman will pick twenty names in assembly tomorrow morning. That's the fairest way to make sure that everyone gets a chance to take part in the rugby – I mean, Pageant. Thanks.'

10.00 a.m. In French
Dear Tansy,
What if he isn't playing this afternoon? What if he doesn't come? And if he does, what shall I say? About Rock-It?

Dear Holly,
He will come. Just say enough about Rock-It to
tempt him — write something alluring on the label of
the present you've got for him.

Dear Tansy,
Like what?

Tansy read the last note, scribbled something on
the back and slipped it across the gangway to
Holly.

'Holly Vine! Give me that piece of paper this
instant!'

Mrs Chapman held out an ink-stained hand.

'Oh, it's nothing, Mrs Chapman, honestly . . .'

'Give!'

Reluctantly Holly passed her the note.

The teacher's eyes scanned Tansy's straggly
writing.

'Rugby's great, rocking's better — how about we give it a
go?'

Mrs Chapman spat the words out with such
force that her false teeth wobbled perilously and
the entire class exploded into uncontrollable mirth.

'Well now, this is most interesting!' she re-
marked. 'I think perhaps you should translate it
into French. Without a single error. Begin.'

'But that's not fair, I —'

'Or perhaps, Holly, you would prefer detention.
This afternoon?'

'No, miss. Sorry, miss.'

Silly old bat.

10.30a.m. In the art room. Putting the finishing touches to the float

'You have to admit,' said Cleo, standing back and admiring their handiwork, 'it does look pretty impressive.'

'I thought you were meant to do something historical,' insisted Trig. 'I mean, it is the Town Pageant after all – you know, eight hundred years since the Dunchester Charter.'

'You're as bad as my dad,' retorted Holly. 'Unless something is so ancient that it is putrefying, you're not interested.'

'Besides, it *is* historical,' said Andy.

'So what's a polystyrene and papier mâché mountain got to do with anything?'

'If you read the banners,' retorted Jade, wiping glue from her hands on to her skirt, 'you'd understand. Look!'

She pointed to the walls, against which were propped pennants and flags, all with brightly coloured lettering.

'Scaling the Heights to Excellence! The Conquest of Everest 1953'

'Finding Footholds to the Future! The Founding of West Green Upper School 1953'

'West Green Upper School – The Pinnacle of Success from 1953 into the future!'

Trig nodded as realization dawned.

'Neat,' he grinned. 'But wasn't Everest more sort of pointy at the top though?'

Holly slammed a paintbrush down on the table and knocked over a pot of water.

'If you haven't got anything constructive to say, just put your name in the bucket and go!'

'OK, OK, sorry!' Trig grinned and dropped a piece of paper into the bucket.

'It's going to be so cool when everyone is actually climbing it,' added Scott, putting the finishing touches to a cling-film and silver-foil icicle.

'Climbing it?' Trig exclaimed. 'How do you mean, climbing it?'

'The sections of the mountain go over a climbing frame and slide,' explained Holly. 'We've cut footholds in the sides so that it looks as if people are really hauling themselves up to the top. We've got ropes and ice picks and everything.'

'My dad's going have to drive the lorry very slowly,' commented Andy, 'just in case someone falls off.'

'I think,' said Trig, fishing the paper out of the bucket, 'I'll pass.'

11.00 a.m. At break. Facing up to a financial crisis

'How much are the Rock-It tickets, anyway?' Holly asked Tansy.

'Fifteen pounds each,' said Tansy.

'WHAT?' Holly almost choked on her crisps. 'I can't afford that much! Two tickets would cost thirty pounds.'

'What about your allowance?' Tansy suggested.

'Spent it already.'

'So can't you get a sub off your mum? That's what I intend to do.'

'Your mum is a normal, generous-hearted human being,' sighed Holly. 'Mine's got all tight-fisted lately and keeps going on about living within my means, and learning a lesson for life.'

'You'll find a way,' Tansy reassured her. 'If you want to go enough, that is.'

'Oh, I want to go,' replied Holly. 'My whole future happiness depends on my being there.'

12.45 p.m. In the cafeteria

'Paul might pay,' said Holly hopefully, biting into her cheese baguette. 'I could hint – very subtly, of course.'

'Holly,' said Tansy.

'What?'

'You don't do subtle,' said Tansy.

2.15 p.m. Worrying

'It's still raining. What if they cancel the match?' Holly stared out of the window, nibbling her fingernail.

'They won't,' said Tansy. 'Rugby players thrive on mud.'

'What if I don't see him?'

'You will,' said Tansy.

'What if he ignores me?'

'Holly?'

'Yes?'

'Can you try to play it cool for once?'

3.30 p.m. Seizing the moment

'He's there!' Holly grabbed Tansy's arm. 'Look, over there. Oh my God! How do I look?'

'Manic,' said Tansy calmly. 'Have you got the present? Did you write the note?'

'Of course I did,' said Holly, still hopping from one foot to the other.

'So get on with it then!' ordered Tansy. 'Hurry up, they're about to go into the changing rooms.'

Holly took a deep breath, flicked her hair behind her ears and ran over to where Paul was deep in conversation with a clutch of Bishop Agnew boys.

'Hi, Paul! How's it going?'

Paul looked up and grinned.

'Oh – hi, Holly. Fine, thanks.'

'Good luck with the match!' she said, slipping her hand into the pocket of her skirt.

'Thanks.' He turned back to his mates. 'OK, now guys, this is how we play it. Jason, I want you out on the wing and –'

'This is for you, Paul!' Holly interrupted, thrusting the parcel into his hand. 'Unwrap it later and follow the instructions. To the letter. I'll be waiting!'

And with that, she parted her lips, let her tongue slide along her teeth, tossed her head again and winked at him.

'I'll be watching the match,' she said as huskily as she could manage. '*Ciao!*'

A burst of ribald banter broke out among Paul's team as Holly strutted off with Tansy hard on her heels.

'Go on, then, open it, Paul!'

'What have you got, Paul?'

'Sexy or what?'

'Just cool it, will you?' Paul's voice rang out behind her. 'We've got a match to play!'

Holly turned to Tansy.

'How did I do?' she asked.

'Fine,' said Tansy, 'apart from one thing.'

'What?'

'The spinach on your teeth.'

'Oh no!'

'Just joking!'

4.25 p.m. Half-time

'Why is everyone giving me funny looks?' Holly asked Tansy and Jade as the teams squatted in the middle of the field.

'I think,' said Jade, 'it's because you keep cheering every time Bishop Agnew score a try.'

'So?'

'So,' said Tansy, 'you're supposed to be shouting for our team.'

'Oh yes,' said Holly. 'I forgot.'

4.35 p.m. Protesting

'Hey, that's not fair!' Holly shrieked. 'Scott knocked Paul over.'

'Holly,' said Jade calmly, 'this is a game of rugby. That's what they do.'

'Well, I don't think it's very nice,' said Holly.

5.00 p.m. A shallow victory

'We won! We won!' Tansy and Jade were jumping up and down on the spot, hugging one another and waving their scarves in the air.

'Scott scored the winning try!' cried Jade. 'Isn't he brilliant?'

'We're into the quarter finals!' exclaimed Tansy. 'Wicked!'

'Does that mean we won't be playing Bishop Ag again?' gasped Holly.

'Of course that's what it means,' said Jade.

'Oh no,' said Holly.

5.10 p.m. Chat-up time

'Bad luck!' Holly touched Paul's arm as he and his mates headed for the school gates.

'Thanks.' Paul smiled half-heartedly and kept walking, his hands stuffed in his pockets.

'You played really well,' she added eagerly.

'I wish,' mumbled Paul.

'I'll see you later then, shall I?'

'Sure.' It came out as muffled grunt. 'Look, I'd better get going.'

A group of burly broad-shouldered guys quickened their pace and caught up with Paul, the tallest slapping him on the shoulder.

'Say, you haven't opened your little pressie yet, have you, Paul?' he teased.

'That's a point,' added another. 'Come on, man, let's see what you've got!'

He grabbed Paul's kitbag and began tossing it between the players.

'Give it to me!' said Paul, but the guys were having too good a time to take any notice.

'This is it!' cried one, pulling the package out of the bag.

Holly looked alarmed.

'I don't want him to open it now,' she hissed. 'Not in front of everyone.'

'I'm not sure,' said Tansy with a sigh, 'that you have much of a choice.'

'Open it, Paul! Open it!'

Paul grinned and tried to look as if he was joining in the fun.

'Later, later,' he said, his face colouring slightly. 'We need a debrief on the match right now.'

'Never mind later,' argued a spotty-faced boy, ripping at the paper. 'What's this?'

He threw the wrapping paper on to the ground and roared with laughter.

'Oh, how sweet! A wickle teddy bear for Pauley Worley!'

Paul lunged at the guy in an attempt to grab the bear.

'And look, it's got a little message on its sweater – what does it say?' The guy peered at it. 'Hug Me!'

The whole team roared with laughter.

'Well, go on then,' they shouted. 'Follow the instructions, she said.'

'Hug her then, Paul! You can do it, man!'

'Don't keep her waiting, Paul!'

Paul, his face reddening by the minute, was about to make another attempt to grab the bear when the Bishop Agnew PE coach strode up to them.

'Will you boys just stop larking around and get into the minibus this minute!' he stormed. 'No one is going home until we've had a post-mortem on that disastrous match! Now move!'

The tall guy tossed the bear at Paul who grabbed it and stuffed it in his pocket before pushing his way on to the minibus, without even one backward glance.

As they walked away, Holly knelt down and picked up the wrapping paper from the ground.

The label was torn and spattered with mud.

'He never got to read my message,' she sighed, turning to Tansy. She took a deep breath.

'Do you think he liked the bear?' she asked.

Tansy chewed her lip.

'Actually,' she said, 'it's rather hard to tell.'

5.30 p.m. Driving Tansy mad

'He's bound to phone, isn't he?' said Holly for the fifth time as she and Tansy turned the corner into Weston Way. 'Or call round even. I mean, he did say he'd see me later. So he will, won't he?'

'Sure to,' agreed Tansy.

'I've got to ask him about Rock-It – he never read the note,' sighed Holly. 'And it was so cool.'

She bit her lip.

'Still – I guess he was so overwhelmed with emotion that he couldn't speak properly at school, wasn't he?'

'Oh yes,' murmured Tansy. 'That'll be it. Absolutely.'

6.45 p.m. 53 Lime Avenue. In a state of shock

Jade stood in the middle of her bedroom and stared in disbelief at her cousin.

'You're a darling and I adore you!' Allegra flung her arms round Jade's neck and hugged her until she could hardly breathe.

Considering, thought Jade, that the only people Allegra usually confessed to adoring were male, six foot three and in possession of quantities of surplus cash, this was a moment to be savoured.

'It's only a shirt,' she grinned. 'Can I take it you are feeling OK now?'

'Never better!' cried Allegra, dancing round the room swigging cola from a plastic bottle and ramming crisps down her throat. 'I don't suppose I could borrow your blue suede desert boots as well, could I?'

'Well . . .'

'Please, please, please!' her cousin implored her. 'I'll never, ever ask you another favour as long as I live.'

'OK then,' sighed Jade, opening her wardrobe and handing them over. 'But if you scuff them or mark them . . .'

'I won't, I promise!'

'So what is all this about?' asked Jade. 'I take it you are going out with Hooray Hugo!'

'Don't call him that!' Allegra's charm evaporated like a snowball in a microwave. 'Why has everyone got it in for him? Just because he knows how to have a good time . . .'

'OK, OK, keep your hair on!' retorted Jade. 'If you're going to yell at me, you can give the boots back.'

Allegra grinned and hugged her again.

'Sorry!' she said, as the doorbell shrilled. 'That'll be him! You're a darling and one day, you'll get a life just like me!'

She squirted perfume all over her hair, took another gulp of her drink and threw the remainder of the crisp packet at Jade.

'See you later!' she trilled. 'Oh – and when Mum gets back from fetching Helen, tell her I've gone to rehearse for the audition. Bye!'

'What time will you be back?' Jade called after her.

But it was too late. Allegra had gone.

7.30 p.m. Being charming

'That was a lovely meal, Mrs Vine,' said Tansy, scraping the last remnants of blackcurrant cheese-cake off her plate. 'We never, ever get smoked salmon or *duck à l'orange* at home!'

Mrs Vine smiled wryly.

'And you wouldn't have had it here, dear, had it not been for Holly's father getting a little carried away round Tesco's,' she said through clenched teeth. 'We still don't have any bread or washing powder, but there seem to be a lot of very smelly continental cheeses in the fridge.'

She looked at Holly's dad who was toying with his dessert.

'Are you going to finish that?' she said, gesturing towards his plate.

'No,' he said wearily. 'I'm exhausted. I've had a hard day.'

'What – resigning, you mean?'

Rupert ignored her pointed remark.

'Doing all that shopping on the way home really took it out of me.'

'Oh really . . .' Angela expostulated.

'I think I'll go up and have a lie down. Nothing's happening this evening, is it?'

'I am going to have a long soak in a hot bath and work out how we are supposed to live on your ridiculously reduced salary,' his wife replied acerbically.

'Angela, don't start,' Holly's father pleaded, jerking his head towards Tansy and pulling a face.

Holly pushed back her chair and beckoned to Tansy.

'We're going up to do homework,' she announced. 'If the phone rings, call me, won't you?'

'Are you expecting anyone?' her mother enquired.

'No,' said Holly casually. 'But I don't want to miss him.'

7.45 p.m. Parental palaver

'Holly! Will you turn that dratted music down!'

Her father threw open her bedroom door and pointed at her stereo.

'I am trying to rest,' he added.

'It's not loud,' moaned Holly.

'It's an assault on the sensibilities of anyone with an ear for music,' he ranted. 'You kids are supposed to be working and you can't do that with this dirge blaring forth and –'

'Dad!' Holly glared at him. 'You're so stuffy! Besides, it's not even late yet.'

'Turn it down! I've got a headache.'

Rupert went puce in the face.

'OK, OK, if I must.' Holly pointed the remote control at the music centre and killed Shiny Vinyl dead in their tracks.

'You do realize we won't be able to work now, don't you?' she said.

'Why not?'

'It's far too quiet.'

7.50 p.m.

'He hasn't rung. Why hasn't he rung?'

'I don't know – what's German for cauliflower?'

Holly clicked her teeth in irritation.

'My life is hanging by a thread and all you can talk about is vegetables,' she retorted.

8.00 p.m. Dealing with the unexpected

Holly was grappling with her maths homework when the doorbell rang.

'That'll be him!' she cried to Tansy. 'He's come round! Stay there.'

She flew down the stairs, stopped halfway and ran back to her bedroom.

'No, come!' she panted, grabbing Tansy by the hand and tearing back to the hall. Fixing what she hoped was a soft and alluring smile on her lips, she yanked open the front door.

'Darling! You –' The smile faded on her lips.

'At last, I am 'ere!' A tall, olive-skinned guy in

the coolest jacket stretched out a hand. 'And you, I think, must be Olly.'

'Holly,' said Holly.

'Who,' breathed Tansy, taking in his gold watch, designer-label chinos and pigskin loafers, 'is this?'

'Search me,' muttered Holly.

'I am José Cavellero,' the guy replied, flinging an Osprey holdall past her into the hallway and smiling to reveal a set of unimaginably white teeth. 'I am to have a room here. It is all arranged, yes?'

He looked expectantly at Holly.

'Actually, no,' gasped Holly. 'I mean, not now. Not yet.'

'But your father – he say on the telephone that everything is – how do you say? Hunky-dory.'

Holly was just trying to imagine her father using such a word when her parents' bedroom door burst open and her father, clad in his scarlet bathrobe and looking less than enchanted with life, blundered down the stairs.

'Holly, how many times do I have to tell you not to let cold air into the house . . . oh!'

He stopped in mid flow and stared open-mouthed at José.

'Mr Vine, I am so happy to meet you!' José held out a hand. 'I am José Cavellero – it is most good of you to 'ave me!'

Rupert swallowed and bit his lip.

'Ah,' he said.

'And I am so sorry for being late in arriving – my plane was delayed.'

'Ah,' said Rupert again.

'I may come in?' José was beginning to look a little confused.

'Of course, of course, old chap!' Mr Vine recovered himself and waved José into the hall. 'Holly, go and fetch your mother.'

Holly was spared the effort by the appearance of her mum at the top of the stairs, a towel wound turban-like round her head.

'This is José, my love,' Holly's father said. Holly realized at once that all was not well. Her father only used such endearments when he was feeling incredibly guilty or wanted an exceptionally big favour. 'You remember I told you he was coming today?'

'I do not,' rejoined her mother, stomping down the stairs. 'You said, Rupert, that someone might be coming some time . . .'

'Oh come, come, my love!' laughed Rupert, rather more loudly than was necessary. 'I remember distinctly saying that I'd had a letter and that José would be with us this evening.'

'Is a problem?' By now José was looking distinctly uncomfortable.

'Of course it's not a problem!' cried Rupert, slapping him on the back. 'Come up and see your room, old chap.'

Holly's mother looked alarmed.

'Rupert,' she muttered, 'that's not a good idea. I haven't had the chance to get things straight.'

Rupert held up a hand and grinned at José.

'Women!' he joked. 'One little thing out of place and they go into a decline. Out of the way, girls. This way, José!'

Angela opened her mouth to protest and then shrugged her shoulders and said nothing.

'I think,' she murmured to Holly and Tansy as they all filed upstairs, 'that all hell is about to be let loose.'

Exactly thirty seconds later. Hell preparing to be let loose

'Here we are!' Rupert threw open the door of Richard's old bedroom and gasped. José leaped back a couple of metres and gulped. Holly and Tansy tried very hard to stifle their giggles and failed utterly.

The floor of the bedroom was piled high with pikestaffs and helmets. In the far corner stood a suit of armour and there was a small cannon propped against the wardrobe. Several flags were draped over the curtain pole and a few leather jerkins hung lopsidedly from hangers on the back of the door. On the chest of drawers stood a couple of small drums and a large musket.

But José wasn't looking at any of those; his eyes were fixed on the bed over which were draped several long dresses. And they were all bloodstained.

Mrs Vine grabbed his arm as he turned pale and staggered backwards.

'What is this?' José gasped, pointing a shaky finger towards the bed.

Angela smiled encouragingly.

'My husband – he's in the Sealed Knot Society, you see . . .'

'Please, what is Silly Not?'

'They fight battles,' said Holly.

'Fight?' José paled and gulped.

'Pretend ones,' added Tansy. 'It's not real blood, you see.'

'Like in pantomime?' José perked up.

'Very much like that,' said Holly's mother dryly. 'Of course, if I had been told you were coming, I would have cleared the room.'

José stepped forward.

'Please, I don't want to make difficulty. I can sleep in here.'

'Oh, no, José,' objected Mrs Vine. 'I don't think so. You are a guest, after all.'

'But I have come here,' insisted José with a dazzling smile, 'to experience normal family life in your country.'

'In which case,' said Holly, 'you have definitely chosen the wrong family.'

'Right!' declared her mother, glaring at her. 'Let's get going. Rupert, start clearing the room. Holly, you'll have to help.'

'I've got homework . . .'

'That's never stopped you wasting time before, so why let it start now? I'll get the sheets.'

Mrs Vine switched instantly into organizing mode.

'José, dear, I expect you'd like a cup of tea. And a sandwich maybe?'

'Yes indeed, thank you. I do have some hunger.'

Mrs Vine nodded.

'Tansy, would you mind awfully taking José downstairs and making him a snack?'

Jose turned and gave Tansy a dazzling smile.

'Oh, but I don't wish to cause you any trouble, Tansy.'

Tansy looked up at him from under her eyelashes.

'Oh, it's no trouble,' she said. 'No trouble at all.'

8.30 p.m. Parental intervention

'Right, let's make a start.' Mrs Vine was rolling up her sleeves when the telephone rang.

'I'll get it,' cried Holly, crashing out of the door and grabbing the extension in her parents' bedroom.

'Oh, Paul – it's you, hi!' She dropped her voice and tried to sound laid back and yet very alluring. 'So what did you think about –'

The receiver was snatched from her hand.

'Paul? Rupert Vine here. Sorry, old boy, but

right now, Holly's tied up. Things to do. I'm sure you two can wait until tomorrow to exchange your sweet nothings! Thanks. Bye.'

He slammed the receiver down.

'DAD! How could you do that? How could you be so rude?' Holly was incandescent with rage.

'Your mother and I need your help,' he said. 'We have a guest in the house.'

'I don't care if the whole Royal Family are taking tea in the lounge,' spat Holly. 'You had no right to do that! Just because you can't bear me to have friends, don't want me to have a life . . .'

'Holly?'

'What?'

'Grow up.'

8.45 p.m. Rapidly becoming besotted
'So what are you doing in England?' Tansy asked, pouring tea into a mug and putting a doorstep-sized cheese sandwich in front of José.

'I have come to study English at the language school,' he said. 'And to do research for my thesis at the university.'

'What's that about?' asked Tansy, cupping her chin in her hands and gazing across the table at him.

'Teen Culture in Great Britain,' he said.

'Fascinating,' breathed Tansy.

'Perhaps you and Olly can help me,' he said brightly.

'Holly's pretty busy these days,' said Tansy hastily. 'But I'd love to.'

'I need to see young people at work and play,' he enthused. 'Where they shop, how they talk, how they spend their money, what music they like . . .'

'Music?'

'Oh yes – it is very important for my project that I experience at first hand the British pop scene.'

'I think,' said Tansy, 'that just possibly this could be arranged.'

'I hope so,' said José. 'Now I am no longer a teenager . . .'

'How old are you?'

'Twenty. And you?'

'Four– practically fifteen,' said Tansy.

'You seem older,' said José. 'More sophisticated than a fifteen-year-old.'

'I do?' Tansy beamed. 'Oh yes. Yes I do. I am. Definitely. Yes.'

9.00 p.m. Removals

'That's it!' sighed Holly's dad, sinking down on to the bed and running a hand wearily over his brow. 'I can't do another thing!'

'Just help me shift this chest of drawers,' asked her mother.

'Can't Holly do it?' Rupert asked. 'I'm whacked.'

'It's too heavy for her,' said Angela. 'It won't take a minute.'

Her husband sighed and grabbed one end. As they began manoeuvring it across the room, he gasped, let go and clutched his arm to his chest.

'What's the matter?' Angela looked irritated.

'My arm,' he said. 'You know, I think I did some real damage to it last weekend. It's hurting more each day.'

Angela frowned.

'You'd better get it looked at then,' she said. 'I expect it's just a pulled muscle; you always were one to make a fuss. Holly, you'll have to do it. Your father's gone into a decline. Again.'

9.30 p.m. Confessions
'Tansy! You'll never believe what my father just did . . .'

Holly crashed into the kitchen.

'Paul rang and . . .' She stopped, eyeing Tansy who was leaning towards José and talking in a most animated manner.

'. . . And then there's Mirage, that's a really cool club . . .'

'Your room is ready now, José,' Holly said. 'You can go up.'

'Thank you,' he said, pushing back his chair.

'I'll show you the way,' said Tansy, leaping to her feet.

'He knows the way,' said Holly. 'He's already been up there.'

José grinned and held up his hand.

'No need, I can manage,' he said. 'And thank you, Tansy, thank you very much. We must talk again. You are so – how is it you say it in English? – clued up.'

Tansy watched him disappear into the hallway and sank back down into her chair with a sigh.

'Oh, Holly,' she said. 'Holly.'

'What?'

Tansy turned to face her with a dreamy smile on her lips.

'Isn't he the most divine guy you have ever seen in your entire life?'

'No,' said Holly. 'Paul's got much nicer eyes. Not that it's likely that he'll ever speak to me again. Do you know –'

'He's twenty,' said Tansy.

'Who?'

'José.'

'Oh, never mind José, I'm telling you about Paul. He rang and he sounded all sort of soft and gooey and then my father came and snatched the phone . . .'

'Holly,' sighed Tansy. 'It's finally happened.'

'What's happened?' retorted Holly impatiently.

'I've fallen in love,' said Tansy.

'Tansy, you've been passionate about Andy for weeks . . .'

'Not him!' retorted Tansy. 'That wasn't love. That was just . . . affection.'

She fondled the dirty coffee mug that José had left on the table.

'I'm in love,' she said, 'with José.'

10.30 p.m. 53 Lime Avenue

'Are you quite sure she said she was going to rehearse for the audition?' Jade's aunt paced the kitchen for the twentieth time. 'She wasn't going on anywhere afterwards?'

Jade shook her head and yawned.

'Oh, where is she?' Paula sighed, biting her fingernails. 'This would have to happen when her father's in Hong Kong. I'm worried out of my mind.'

At that moment, there was the sound of a key turning in the front door. Paula rushed along the hall.

'Allegra darling! Thank goodness! Where have you been?'

She stopped as the tall figure of Hugo loomed behind her daughter.

'Hello, Mrs Webb,' he said, stepping into the hall without being asked. 'I've brought Allegra home – she's not feeling too well.'

'There you are!' exclaimed Paula. 'I knew you shouldn't have gone out tonight – you're not over that bug. I thought you were rehearsing.'

'I was,' said Allegra hurriedly. 'Hugo came to watch.'

Paula sighed.

'And you've got the auditions on Thursday. Oh dear, oh dear.'

Allegra yawned and leaned against the wall.

'Don't fuss, Mum,' she said. 'I'll be fine in the morning.'

'You wish,' grinned Hugo.

'What?' asked Paula.

'It's a nasty bug that's going around, Mrs Webb,' he said solemnly. 'Me and my mates have all had it.'

'You have? Maybe that's where she picked it up then,' mused Paula.

'I guess it must be,' he said solemnly. 'Sorry, Mrs Webb.'

'It's not your fault, Hugo,' said Paula. 'These things happen. Darling, you look so pale.'

Hugo winked at Jade.

'She will survive, you know,' he said. 'Anyway, must dash – take care, Lego.'

He waved and strode off down the path.

'I do wish he wouldn't call you that,' sighed Paula, slipping an arm round Allegra's shoulder. 'I'll get you a hot drink.'

'No!' Allegra protested, pushing her mother away and heading up the stairs. 'I don't want anything. I just want to go to sleep.'

'Did the rehearsal go well?' Paula called after her. 'You think you'll be up to scratch for the audition.'

'Yes, yes, yes!' snapped Allegra. 'It was fine. I'll be fine. Just stop fussing.'

Jade turned and kissed her aunt.

'Don't worry,' she said. 'I'll make sure she's OK.'

Which, she thought, following her cousin up the stairs, is a pretty dumb thing to say, considering it's pretty obvious to anyone with half a brain that she's not OK at all.

TUESDAY

2.00 a.m. Nightmare city

'No! No, please! I don't want to! No!'

Jade shot out of bed before she was hardly awake and shook Allegra's shoulder.

'It's OK, Legs, you're dreaming. Wake up. It's all right.'

'What? No! Oh!' Allegra eyes flew open and Jade saw that her eyelashes were wet with tears.

Jade switched on the bedside light and put an arm round her cousin.

'What was it? What were you dreaming?'

For just the briefest second, Allegra hesitated. Then she pulled away, and turned on to her side.

'Nothing, all right? Oh, my head – it's killing me!'

Jade bit her lip. Maybe Allegra really was ill – she knew people had hideous nightmares when they ran a fever, and she had promised Paula that she'd keep an eye on her cousin. She put a hand on Allegra's forehead. Allegra jerked her head away.

'Don't! Just leave me alone, OK? I'm fine.'

Jade sighed and climbed back into bed. But she didn't go straight back to sleep. She lay on her back, straining her ears. And because she had once been so very good at doing it herself, she knew that Allegra had the corner of the pillowcase stuffed in her mouth and was doing her best to stifle her sobs.

6.15 a.m. In pursuit of beauty

'Holly! Holly, wake up!' Tansy shook her friend's shoulder in exasperation.

'What? Who? Whaddyawant?' Holly opened one eye and pulled the duvet more tightly round her.

'Can I borrow some shampoo? And where do you keep your hairdryer? Oh, and can I have some of that lilac shimmer nail polish? I'll pay you back.'

Holly rolled over and glanced at her bedside clock.

'Tansy!' she exploded. 'It's only a quarter-past six. What's wrong with you?'

Tansy slumped down on the end of Holly's bed.

'I couldn't sleep,' she said. 'I keep thinking about him – the way he looked at me, the sound of his voice, the little half moons on his fingernails . . .'

'Oh puhleese!' Holly grinned and sat up, hunching her knees under chin. 'Are you being serious? You really like him? You're not having me on?'

'I love him,' sighed Tansy.

'But you don't even know him!' reasoned Holly. 'And anyway, he's too old for you.'

'There's only five years' difference,' protested Tansy.

'Practically six,' said Holly.

'So what?' retorted Tansy. 'Loads of women marry men older than them.'

'Oh, it's marriage now, is it?' teased Holly. 'Anyway, he's probably got a string of girlfriends in Spain. He's not going to be interested in a fourteen-year-old.'

Tansy tossed her head.

'He said I was sophisticated,' she said.

'Clearly, his English does need improving,' grinned Holly. 'He probably meant soppy.'

Tansy threw her a steely look.

'Shampoo,' she said. 'Now.'

7.00 a.m. Being charming

'Hi, Mrs Vine!' Tansy poked her head round the kitchen door. 'Can I help?'

'Tansy! Not another early bird! I wish my family were as good at getting up in the mornings.'

Tansy tried to look unconcerned.

'So – who else is up?'

'I am!' José appeared in the doorway, clutching a map. 'I am trying to find where is the language college.'

'I'll show you,' said Tansy eagerly, grabbing the

map and spreading it out on the table. 'Look, we're here, in Weston Way, and the language college is there, in Lansdowne Gardens.'

'But this is very far!' José looked alarmed. 'There is a bus, yes?'

'Oh yes,' interjected Mrs Vine, cracking eggs into the frying pan.

'No,' said Tansy at the same instant. 'That is, yes – but it's much nicer to walk. I could go with you – show you some of the sights of Dunchester on the way.'

She threw him what she hoped was an irresistibly dazzling smile.

'What sights?' Holly burst through the door, her hair hanging damply round her shoulders. 'A few measly castle ruins and a shopping centre that doesn't even have a Warehouse in it.'

'And the river, and the cathedral and . . .' Tansy's voice trailed off as she tried desperately to think of more noteworthy attractions.

'I would like this very much!' exclaimed Jose. 'And you can show me where the young people – how is it? – hang out. That is the right expression, no? Hang out?'

'Quite right,' interrupted Mrs Vine. 'Hanging out is about all half of them are fit for.'

'Excuse me?' José was already fishing for his phrase book.

'Ignore her,' ordered Holly. 'She's just trying to be clever.'

Tuesday

7.15 a.m. In high dudgeon

'Allegra!' Jade swung round from the wardrobe and faced her cousin. 'You've ruined my boots!'

She waved the stained boots in Allegra's face.

'Stop it!' Allegra groaned, turning her face away. 'I'll clean them – it's no big deal!'

'Yes it is!' shouted Jade, close to tears. 'What were you doing in them, for heaven's sake?'

Allegra tossed her head.

'Someone spilt an orange juice on them,' she said, snatching them from Jade's hand. 'I said, I'll clean them, OK?'

She grabbed her bathrobe and headed for the door, tossing the boots on her bed as she went.

'I will, Jade, honestly. Promise.'

After she had gone, Jade picked up the boots. They were in a revolting mess. She sniffed the pale blue suede.

And pulled back.

Something had certainly been spilt on the boots. And she wasn't at all sure that it was simply an orange juice.

7.40 a.m. On the case

'I'm ready!' Tansy, wearing a considerable quantity of mascara and her new clogs, stood beaming at José. 'Catch you later, Holly!'

'Hang on!' Holly protested. 'I'll come with you.'

'No!' Tansy shook her head. 'You need to see Paul, remember? I'll catch you at school.'

'But what about Andy? You always call for him and –'

'I do not wish to be any trouble,' said José. 'Who is this Andy?'

'He's her –' began Holly.

'Just some kid in my class,' finished Tansy hastily. 'Come on, José. Let's hit the road!'

8.00 a.m.

'Steve! Wait a moment! Steve!' Holly belted up the road and grabbed Paul's twin brother by the arm. 'Where's Paul?'

'Oh, it's you!' Steve rejoined. 'He's running late. He hasn't left yet.'

'Great!' exclaimed Holly. 'I'll run back to your house and catch him.'

She turned.

'I don't think that's a very good idea,' said Steve. 'I'm not sure that he wants to see you, actually.'

Holly laughed.

'Which shows just how much you know,' she said smugly. 'Paul is desperate to talk to me. He can't wait!'

She tossed her hair over her shoulder and set off down the road.

'Holly . . .'

'Get lost,' she said.

8.05 a.m.

She bumped into Paul as he came out of his front gate.

'Hi, darling,' she said with a broad smile. 'Sorry about my father.'

'That's OK,' he said.

'So, did you like the bear? Are you ready to . . .' She paused for dramatic effect. 'To carry out the instructions?'

She waited expectantly for the hug.

Paul coughed and swallowed.

'That's what I wanted to talk to you about,' he began.

'Talk?' said Holly, daringly running her hand through the curl of hair at the back of his neck. 'Why talk?'

Paul pulled away.

'It was a bit . . . well, you know . . .'

'What?'

'I mean, it was a lovely present and everything,' he said hastily, casting an anxious glance up and down the road. 'Really nice of you but . . .'

'But what?'

'Well, it was embarrassing,' he said with a rush, his neck reddening. 'I mean, what with me being captain and all the guys around.'

'They were pretty out of order,' Holly agreed.

'Yes, but – well, those kind of things should be done in private, shouldn't they?' Paul stammered. 'I don't like it when you – when you come on strong in public.'

Holly dropped her gaze.

'I thought you liked me,' she said dully.

'I do, I really do!' Paul insisted. 'But I don't want – you know.'

'Don't want what?' There was an edge to Holly's voice.

'Everyone being in on it,' finished Paul.

Holly breathed a sigh of relief.

'You mean,' she said, slipping her hand into his, 'you want us to be a private thing – a sort of secret love?'

'I guess,' he said somewhat doubtfully.

'So – if I suggested that we went to Rock-It . . .'

'What?'

'Rock-It – it's at The Bowl on Saturday with mega good bands, and DJs and everything.'

She smiled up at him alluringly.

'And we could spend hours together,' she added.

'Can't afford it,' Paul gabbled hastily. 'I'm totally skint.'

Holly beamed at him.

'Oh, don't worry about that!' she said airily. 'It's my treat.'

'Oh,' said Paul. 'Well then, I guess – well, thanks.'

After he had gone, Holly hugged herself in delight. And then began worrying. She'd got Paul to agree – but she hadn't got thirty pounds and she hadn't got permission to go. But it would be OK. Something would turn up. It had to. Love conquered all, the books said so.

8.15 a.m. Liquid assets?

'Hey, Mum, there are no more bottles of cola left!' Allegra peered into the cupboard. 'I need one for my packed lunch.'

Paula sighed.

'There are plenty of cans in the fridge,' she said. 'Grab one of those.'

'I don't want a can!' snapped Allegra. 'I want a bottle.'

'Why?' asked Jade, who was still feeling miffed about her boots. 'What possible difference does it make?'

'All the difference in the world, actually,' said Allegra. 'I get very thirsty rehearsing and singers need to keep their throats lubricated. Cans go flat once they've been opened.'

'Oh darling, of course!' cried Paula. 'How thoughtless of us! Tell you what – there's an empty lemonade bottle in the larder. If I tip a couple of cans into that, would that do?'

'Perfect,' said Allegra. 'Thanks, Mum. You're a star.'

8.20 a.m. Begging a favour

'You know I've got this audition? In London? On Thursday?' Allegra blurted out as she and Jade walked down the path.

Jade nodded.

'Yes,' she said. 'Are you excited?'

'No. Yes. Oh, I don't know.' She took a deep

breath. 'Anyway, will you come with me?'

'Me? Come with you? But it's a school day,' Jade protested.

'Please, Jade. Please.'

Jade was speechless. Please was not a word Allegra was accustomed to use, and especially not in conversations with her cousin.

'I can't, Allegra, it's . . .'

To Jade's horror, Allegra's eyes filled with tears.

'I hate you! Do you know that? I hate you!'

And with that, her cousin turned on her heel and ran up the road.

8.55 a.m. Reporting back

'You didn't call for me.' Andy, panting hard, caught up with Tansy in the locker room. 'I waited for ages – what happened?'

'Oh, I had things to do,' she said airily. 'Sorry.'

Andy looked dejected.

'I wanted to talk to you about Dad,' he said.

'Oh, right.' Tansy looked distracted.

'He got back really late last night,' Andy went on, 'and he was in a foul mood. I mean really, really bad.'

'How do you mean?' asked Tansy, gently stroking the palm of her left hand which José had held as they crossed the main road.

'Well, I asked where he'd been and he just said he'd tell me when I needed to know, which wasn't now. And then he stormed into his study and slammed the door.'

'Weird,' said Tansy. 'So you never found out about the phone call?'

Andy shook his head.

'I guess it can't have been Mum,' he said sadly. 'He couldn't keep something like that a secret all this long, could he?'

'No,' said Tansy, gazing into the middle distance with a dreamy look on her face.

'But one good thing came out of it,' added Andy, touching her arm.

'Mm. Oh, sorry, what did you say?'

'I said,' emphasized Andy, 'that there was a good side to it. Just before I went to bed, I said I was strapped for cash. I had to say it three times because he just wasn't with it at all, and then guess what?'

'What?' sighed Tansy.

'He just waved me away and told me to help myself from his wallet and leave him in peace. So I did.'

He waited for Tansy to burst into exclamations of delight. Nothing happened.

'I got thirty pounds,' he said. 'Thirty quid.' He shouted the last two words into her ear.

'OK, OK, that's great. Good.'

'So, I can take you to Rock-It,' he grinned. 'What do you say to that?'

'Oh,' said Tansy.

Andy stared at her.

'Is that all you can say?' he snapped. 'You go on and on about how much you want to go, and then I say I'll take you and –'

'Sorry,' said Tansy. 'That's great. Honestly. Only someone else –'

'Someone else what?'

Tansy looked at his eager face and felt just a little bit guilty.

'Nothing,' she said. 'That's cool. Really cool.'

9.00 a.m. Filing into Assembly

'I thought that was really off of you,' snapped Holly to Tansy. 'Going off with José like that and dumping me in it.'

'How do you mean?' Tansy looked genuinely baffled.

'My mum got on her high horse – saying stuff like, why can't you be as helpful as Tansy? Tansy has such charming manners. I'm sure Tansy doesn't speak to her mother the way you do . . . on and on and on.'

Tansy grinned.

'I am rather adorable, aren't I?' she giggled. 'José thinks so.'

'He said you were adorable?'

Tansy pulled a face.

'Well, not exactly,' she admitted. 'He said I had a cute nose.'

Holly raised her eyebrows.

'I always said these Mediterranean types were too oily for their own good.'

9.20 a.m. Storming out of Assembly in a huff

'Well, that's just terrific!' Holly shouted, elbowing her way past a crowd of Year Eights. 'Twenty people on the float and I'm not one of them!'

'Never mind,' said Cleo soothingly. 'It'll be fun running alongside collecting the money.'

'Oh, it's all right for you,' returned Holly, thumping her way up the stairs to the Science lab. 'You're on the float. So's Jade. And Tansy. I'm doomed to be left out. As usual.'

'I don't know what you're getting in such a state about,' reasoned Jade. 'At least you're allowed to go to Rock-It. Auntie Paula seems to think that all pop concerts are hotbeds of vice and depravity!'

'Ah,' said Holly, 'I haven't exactly sorted that one out yet.'

'I'm going,' said Tansy smugly. 'Win or not. With Jos . . . Andy.'

'And your mum doesn't mind?' Jade looked amazed.

'She doesn't know yet,' admitted Tansy. 'But she can't refuse. She used to go to loads of pop festivals when she was younger. She was a hippy – you know, flower power and wandering round the countryside talking to trees. She doesn't have a leg to stand on.'

'You are lucky!' sighed Jade. 'I mean Man Overboard are just the funkiest sound out – and as for Damien in Shiny Vinyl . . .'

She closed her eyes and performed a mock swoon against the wall.

'Jade Williams!' Mrs Bainbridge's ample chest had encountered the fainting Jade. 'Pull yourself together and get to your next lesson. Now.'

11.00 a.m. At break

'There has to be a way!' Holly bit into her apple. 'Somehow I have to get enough money to get the tickets or else Paul won't come.'

'Holly,' sighed Tansy. 'Can't you just ask your parents to sub you? Then we might get a bit of peace round here?'

'Oh charming,' said Holly.

And made a mental note to be utterly creepy to both parents that evening.

11.45 a.m.

Cleo, Trig, Tansy, Andy, Jade and Holly were ambling across the school yard with half of Year Nine when Mrs Bainbridge bustled up wearing her officious look.

'Now, everyone, stand back! Out of the way! Clear a path, please!'

They turned to see a huge, forty-foot flatback trailer being slowly reversed across the yard towards the Art Block.

'Hey, Andy, isn't that your dad?' Scott asked. 'Is this the lorry for the float?'

'I guess so,' said Andy. 'At least he's remembered.'

'It's huge,' commented Cleo. 'You can get loads of people on that.'

'Except me,' sighed Holly.

'Move along now, Nine-S!' cried Mrs Braithwaite. 'Snip, snap!'

Tansy touched Andy's arm.

'Say, is Spanish one of our options for Year Ten?'

Andy nodded.

'Yes,' he said. 'Why?'

'Oh, nothing,' said Tansy.

12.45 p.m. In the cafeteria

'I could sell my hair,' said Holly thoughtfully, running her fingers through her brown locks. 'How much do you think I'd get for it?'

'Holly,' said Tansy. 'Get real.'

2.45 p.m. Bright ideas

'Hey!' screeched Holly in the middle of an experiment. 'I've got it!'

'If you are not very careful, Miss Vine,' thundered Mr Grubb, 'what you will get will be a detention for disrupting the class. Now get on with your work.'

'Tell you later,' whispered Holly with a grin on her face. 'I've got it sussed!'

3 p.m. Not so bright

While her daughter was feeling triumphant over a Bunsen burner, Mrs Vine was sitting at the kitchen table, eating far too much flapjack and feeling fed up with the world at large.

'Angela, I'm back!' The back door flew open and Clarity Meadows, Tansy's mum, hurtled into the kitchen. 'You don't mind me just marching in, do you, only I've come for Tansy's bags and . . . Angela! What's wrong?'

'You want a list?' Mrs Vine smiled up at Clarity ruefully. 'I have a Spaniard in my spare bedroom . . .'

'What?'

'. . . A husband who has just chucked in his job . . .'

'No!'

'. . . And my HRT definitely isn't working. The boiler's gone on the blink again and as for Holly . . .'

'What's wrong with Holly?' Clarity looked alarmed.

'Wrong? She's a typical fourteen-year-old. That's what's wrong.'

'I think,' said Clarity, helping herself to a large slice of flapjack, 'that you'd better start at the beginning.'

'OK,' said Mrs Vine. 'Do you have a few hours?'

3.15 p.m. The best idea to date

'So what was the big idea?' queried Tansy as they piled their books into their kit bags.

'This pop concert – it's for charity, right?' said Holly.

'Yes – so?'

'So – my parents can't refuse to sub me the cash, can they? I mean, there's my mum, spending her whole life forgetting to go shopping because she's counselling single mums or making cheese sandwiches for the homeless. And now my dad's gone mental and keeps muttering about running this museum and getting disadvantaged kids to learn to love history.'

'Weird,' agreed Tansy.

'So they have to say yes to me supporting a charity, don't they?'

Tansy looked at her admiringly.

'Do you know,' she said, 'I think you may have cracked it.'

'I know,' said Holly proudly. 'Didn't I always say I would?'

3.25 p.m. Very impressed

'Now that,' said Jade, pointing round the corner of the Art block, 'is something else.'

'Wow!' Scott looked impressed. During the afternoon, the float had been fitted out. The mountain stood in the middle, ice picks hanging from its protruberances. Fake snow lay all over the

74

trailer, with two stuffed penguins and a rather moth-eaten-looking walrus for added effect. All round the edge of the lorry hung the posters and banners and on top of the cab was the crest of West Green Upper School with its motto 'Aim to Achieve'.

'Impressive, isn't it?' Mr Grubb was grappling with a tarpaulin. 'Now run and find a few of your mates to help with this, will you? We don't want a downpour in the night to ruin all your handiwork for Open Day.'

'Never mind Open Day,' muttered Scott. 'It's Saturday night that matters.'

'Afternoon, Scott. The Pageant is in the afternoon,' said Mr Grubb.

'Oh yes, that too,' said Scott and went to fetch his mates.

3.45 p.m. Happy reunions?

Tansy glanced at her watch and sighed. It would be another half hour before there was even the remotest chance of bumping into José on his way home from college.

'I'll walk to your house if you like,' she said to Andy, turning with him into Fishponds Road.

'Cool,' said Andy. And suddenly stopped and stood stock still, his eyes following her gaze. He took his spectacles off, wiped them on his sleeve and replaced them. And still he stared.

The woman in the blue dress opened the gate

and stood hesitantly on the pavement. Slowly she raised a hand in a wave.

'Andy?'

Andy's mouth opened in a great cry.

'MUM!' he cried. 'Mum!'

And he flew off down the road, his open kitbag spilling books and papers on to the pavement. Tansy stooped and picked them up. She was about to run after him when she saw him throw himself into his mother's arms.

Biology, she thought, can wait.

5.00 p.m. The model daughter returns
Holly burst into the kitchen and gave her mother a big hug.

'Hi, Mum! Had a good day?'

'Well . . .'

'You look tired, Mum. Why don't you sit down and I'll make us both a nice cup of tea? And then maybe you'd like me to get the supper started?'

Her mother sank into a chair.

'Holly, are you feeling all right?'

'Me? Fine!' smiled Holly sweetly. 'I'm just concerned about you, that's all.'

5.15 p.m. Claiming her reward
'Mum?'

'Yes, Holly?'

'I was wondering . . .'

'I thought you might be,' smiled her mother resignedly. 'Go on.'

'Well,' said Holly, 'could I have next month's allowance now?'

'No.'

'What do you mean, no?' Holly's good mood evaporated instantly.

'Holly, today is the sixth of the month. You get your allowance on the first. Where, in the name of goodness, has it all gone?'

Holly shrugged.

'I have expenses,' she said loftily. 'I had to buy a bra that cost fifteen pounds . . .'

'Fifteen pounds! For a bra!' her mother ex-claimed. 'What's it made of? Silk? You can get perfectly adequate bras for eight pounds in M and S.'

'I need uplift,' said Holly.

'You need a brain transplant,' retorted her mother. 'So where's the rest of it gone?'

'Oh well, if you're going to demand a set of accounts,' shouted Holly, 'forget it.'

5.20 p.m. Grovelling
'Mum?'

'Yes, Holly.'

'Sorry.'

'Apology accepted.'

'So I can have some money?'

Her mother sighed and picked up her handbag.

'What's it for?' she said.

'There's this pop concert,' Holly said, holding out her hand.

The handbag was snapped shut and slammed back on the table.

'A pop concert!' Mrs Vine sounded as if Holly had suggested departing for the planet Zog on an alien spaceship. 'You have to be joking. Do you honestly think I'd let you go off to something like that on your own?'

Holly counted to ten and willed herself to stay calm.

'I won't be on my own,' she said. 'All my mates will be with me.'

Angela frowned.

'And their parents don't mind?'

'Oh no,' said Holly airily. 'They're all in favour.'

She could see that her mother was hesitating.

'It's for charity,' she said, playing her winning card.

'Well . . .' said her mother and then pulled herself together. 'You can't. There's the Pageant to think of.'

'The parade will be over by three,' said Holly. 'And the concert doesn't start till five. There's plenty of time to get to The Bowl.'

'The Bowl?' Angela's eyes widened. 'At The Bowl?'

Holly nodded.

'No,' said her mother. 'Definitely and finally no.

The last time they had an event there, people got arrested.'

'You got arrested dressed as a white rabbit last summer,' Holly reminded her. 'And that was in the middle of town.'

'That was for a good cause,' said her mother, looking mildly embarrassed.

'So is this,' claimed Holly triumphantly. 'Please?'

'No, Holly,' said her mother. 'I'm only saying this because I care about you.'

'That,' said Holly sullenly, 'is what everyone says when they don't want their kids to get a life.'

5.25 p.m. 3 Plough Cottages, Cattle Hill.
Mum in clover

'Oh, you're back!' Tansy slammed the back door and threw her school bag into the corner of the kitchen. 'What's that?'

Tansy pointed to a cellophane-wrapped packet in her mother's hands.

'Hello, mother darling, and did you have a good time in Torquay?' commented Clarity teasingly.

'Sorry!' Tansy planted a kiss on her mum's cheek. 'It's a rose!'

'Yes,' sighed Clarity.

'From the ghastly Lawrence, I take it?' Tansy had hoped that when her mother refused to move in with Lawrence Murrin, that would be an end to their relationship, but, sadly, he still hovered around, taking her out for dinner and generally being a pain.

'No, actually, it's not,' said Clarity. 'I've met someone else.'

'Oh joy,' sighed Tansy.

'His name is Henry, and he's a rose grower . . .'

'Oh yawn, another horticultural type.' Tansy rolled her eyes.

'And he's quite a bit older than me,' said Clarity with a rush.

'That's OK,' said Tansy. 'I've come to the conclusion that older men have a lot more to offer.'

She ignored the expression of amazement on her mother's face and carried on.

'Now listen, Mum, I'm going to a pop concert on Saturday. It's at –'

'The Bowl? The big one? You're not!'

'Now look, Mum, I'm quite old enough –'

'Of course you are, that's not what I mean,' cried her mum. 'I didn't know you had a ticket.'

Tansy nodded.

'Andy's getting them this evening,' she said. 'But actually –'

Clarity clapped her hands.

'I must get mine,' she said.

'You what?'

'Well,' her mother continued, 'it's a great line-up of bands and it's been years since I went to anything like that – Henry would love it.'

She beamed at Tansy.

'He's very hip for sixty,' she added.

'Sixty?' Tansy gasped. 'You said old, but I didn't think you meant senile.'

'We can go in a foursome,' she said. 'Wouldn't that be cool?'

'No,' said Tansy. 'It would not.'

9 p.m. On the phone to Holly

'Can you imagine? At their age? It's obscene.' Tansy dropped her voice as her mother walked past.

'No, it's not,' Holly said from the other end. 'It's brill.'

'You wouldn't say that if it was your mother,' began Tansy.

'Use your head,' insisted Holly. 'If your mum goes, she can drive us there. And then all the other parents have to let us go. They'll all be totally laid back about it if your mum is in charge.'

'Which just goes to show,' said Tansy, 'how misguided some people can be.'

WEDNESDAY

7.30 a.m. In poetic mood

'What,' mused Holly out loud, sucking the end of her roller ball pen, 'rhymes with passion? Dashin', mashin', fashion? That's it! Fashion!'

She was scrawling a few words inside a fluorescent-pink card when her mother burst into the kitchen.

'Look, you'll have to get breakfast for José and your father – I've got to rush out. There's been a crisis at the Women's Hostel.'

She grabbed her handbag from the Welsh dresser.

'Tell your father to expect me when he sees me,' she said. 'I think it's going to be a very long day.'

She paused.

'Holly, have you heard one word that I have been saying?'

Holly looked up and smiled sweetly.

'Oh yes, Mum,' she said, thinking that Fate had played straight into her hands by leaving her alone with her dad. He was such a soft touch when Holly got him to herself. 'Have a nice day.'

7.35 a.m. On Paul's doorstep

Holly stood on Paul's doorstep, scanning the poem she had composed inside her heart-shaped card.

> *You are my dearest secret love*
> *The apple of my eye*
> *If you should ask it, sweet, of me,*
> *I would lie down and die.*
> *But I would rather live than die*
> *And now I've found a way*
> *That you and I can be alone*
> *For hours on Saturday.*
> *To hold your hand and kiss your face*
> *In unrelenting passion,*
> *Tell me you're as keen, my love,*
> *In your usual loving fashion.*

That last bit's not right, she thought with a sigh, and I can't find an envelope that will fit. But it will have to do. I know it will touch him. It is very moving.

7.40 a.m. Back home

Holly had just got back to the house and poured herself a glass of orange juice when her father shuffled into the kitchen.

'Hi, Dad. Mum's gone out. She says get your own breakfast and she'll see you whenever.'

She was about to mention Rock-It when she saw her dad flinch and slump into a chair.

'Are you OK?'

Rupert nodded slowly.

'Yes, I just feel a bit woozy, that's all. Nothing a strong cup of coffee won't sort. Where's she gone?'

Holly frowned.

'Can't remember. Some crisis somewhere or other, I think.'

'Doubtless,' sighed her father. 'Your mother loves a good crisis.'

7.45 a.m. Trying it on

'Mum,' said Cleo, shoving her lunch box into her school bag. 'There's this concert on Saturday at The Bowl.'

'Really, darling?'

'And I wondered if you could lend me the money for a ticket.'

'Oh, I should think so, sweetheart,' cooed her mother.

'You think WHAT?' Cleo's stepfather almost dropped the pile of plates he was loading into the dishwasher. 'You must be out of your mind.'

'Why?'

'Pop concerts – at her age?' he argued. 'Drugs everywhere, fights breaking out, probably no crowd control whatsoever . . .'

He was going quite purple in the face.

'You're right, Roy, of course you are,' said Diana hastily. 'Plenty of time for that sort of thing when you're grown up, angel.'

'If,' said Cleo with a sigh, 'I last that long.'

7.50 a.m. DIY in the kitchen

'I have come,' José announced brightly, striding into the kitchen. 'Ready for the magnificent English breakfast again.'

'Bad luck,' said Holly. 'Mum's out on a mission of mercy.'

'Please, what is mercy?'

'French for thank you,' grinned Holly.

'Sorry, I do not understand,' frowned José.

'Ignore her, José,' said Mr Vine. 'She's just trying to be clever. Would you like bacon and eggs?'

'Oh yes, very much!' José beamed.

'Holly?' her father looked at her expectantly.

She opened a cupboard.

'There,' she said, 'is the frying pan. It's all yours'

7.55 a.m. Visiting

'. . . So I just thought I'd pop round and say thank you again to Mrs Vine for having me to stay.'

Tansy gave Holly's father her most winning smile.

'I'm sorry to have missed her,' she said. 'Oh, José, I didn't see you there!'

'Much,' muttered Holly.

'Ah, Tansy!' José swung round from the cooker where he was massacring two perfectly innocent eggs. 'It is so good to see you again. I have thought about what you said yesterday.'

Tansy looked at him with wide eyes.

'And indeed, I will be – how is it said? – over the moon to come with you on Saturday. You are just the very person I would want to be with on such an occasion.'

Holly looked at Tansy in amazement.

'But you said you were going with –'

'Terrific!' interrupted Tansy hastily. 'That will be so cool. Come on, Holly, we must fly. Enjoy your eggs, José.'

He waved a wooden spoon by way of farewell.

'And Tansy,' he called.

'Yes?'

'Tonight you will come and help me?'

'I think I can fit you in,' said Tansy.

8.00 a.m. Getting the facts

'And just where are you going tonight?' demanded Holly as they walked to school.

'To Mirage,' smiled Tansy. 'José wants to see where it's all at.'

'I'll come if you like,' said Holly.

'I don't like,' said Tansy.

'Charming,' said Holly.

9.00 a.m. In Registration

'Tansy Meadows! A word, please.' Miss Partridge beckoned from across the room. 'Have you any idea whether Andy Richards is ill? He's never late for Registration as a rule.'

Tansy bit her lip.

'I don't think he'll be here,' she said. 'Something came up at home last night.'

Miss Partridge nodded and made a mark in her record book.

'What came up?' asked Holly.

'You know his mum went missing,' said Tansy. 'Well, she's home.'

'Really? That's terrific! I bet Andy is over the moon.'

Tansy nodded.

'And hopefully, the joyous reunion will keep him occupied for days,' she said.

'Tansy,' said Holly, 'you're not about to dump him, are you?'

'Only,' said Tansy, 'in the nicest possible way.'

10.15 a.m. At the end of first period

'Andy!' Holly charged down the corridor. 'Tansy didn't think you'd be coming to school today. Are you OK?'

'Sure. Why?'

'Well, she told me. About your mum being back and everything. I'm really, really pleased for you.'

Andy nodded slowly and smiled.

'Yeah. Thanks.'

Holly was itching to find out more.

'So – I mean, is she OK? What happened?'

Andy said nothing.

'Or perhaps you don't want to talk about it,' ventured Holly.

'No,' he said. 'I don't.'

11.30 a.m. Being very bored by the War of the Roses

Holly leaned across the table and prodded Tansy.

'Have you spoken to Andy yet?' she asked.

Tansy shook her head.

'Only he doesn't seem very happy,' said Holly, 'considering his mum's back and everything.'

'Doesn't he?' murmured Tansy. 'Do you think I should wear my black hipsters tonight or the suede minidress?'

11.55 a.m. Forward planning

'If I tell my dad that your mum is taking us to the concert, he's bound to let me go,' mused Holly. 'Isn't he?'

'Sure to,' said Tansy. 'Parents don't like other parents to think they are uptight and uncool. Believe me, he'll be a pushover.'

'I can't wait to be alone with Paul,' sighed Holly. 'Unseen and unnoticed.'

Tansy sighed.

'You'll be out of luck then, won't you?' she said

with a grin. 'There will only be another nineteen thousand nine hundred and ninety-eight people hanging around.'

12.15 p.m. Toying with a cheeseburger
Tansy flopped down on the bench beside Andy and took his biology book from her bag.

'You dropped this last night,' she said. 'Sorry about the muddy bit.'

'Thanks.' Andy slid it along the table and continued picking bits of cheese out of his burger.

'So did you have a big celebration then?' Tansy asked. 'With your mum?'

Andy shook his head.

'Not really,' he said, swallowing hard. 'Me and Ricky talked to Mum for bit and then she and Dad went off upstairs and –'

'Oh, wayhay! Get them!'

'Not that!' spat Andy. 'You just make fun of everything, don't you? Well, it's not funny. None of it. OK?'

He pushed back the bench, hurled his burger into the pedal bin and stomped out of the cafeteria.

For just a moment, Tansy felt very guilty. And then she turned her attention to the more serious matter of which nail polish to wear for José.

3.15 p.m. Ready reckoning
Holly stood in the locker room counting the money in her purse.

'Hey, Tansy, fancy going shopping on the way home? I need to get Paul a pressie.'

Tansy shook her head.

'I've got to get home, wash my hair, curl my eye-lashes, varnish my nails ... Besides,' she added with a frown, 'you've just given Paul a present.'

'I know,' said Holly, 'but I realize now it wasn't subtle enough. I need to get him something under-stated yet wildly romantic.'

'I thought you were broke,' said Tansy.

'I am,' sighed Holly. 'How subtle can you be for one pound seventy-five?'

3.25 p.m. At the school gates

Tansy was deciding whether to catch the bus or risk a downpour and walk home when Andy came panting up to her.

'Walk home?' he said.

Tansy glanced at her watch.

'I'm in a tearing hurry,' she said. 'Sorry.'

'We can walk fast,' offered Andy.

Tansy nodded.

'I guess you can't wait to get home, now your mum's back,' she said.

Andy chewed his lip.

'I used to dream about her coming home, you know,' he said. 'Only now she has, it's not like the dream at all.'

'What do you mean? Quick, cross over here before the lights change.'

They dashed across the road.

'Well,' Andy panted as they reached the other side, 'Dad's hardly speaking to her, Mum keeps bursting into tears, and then . . .'

His voice trailed off.

'What?'

'This morning she was sitting at the table, really pale and with big black lines under eyes. Not eating or anything.'

Tansy said nothing.

'And just before I left for school I heard Dad say she had to go to the doctor and see if he couldn't sort her out before . . .'

He paused.

'What?' she asked wearily. 'Before what?'

'Before it was too late,' he choked. 'Tansy, I think my mum's ill. Really, really ill.'

3.45 p.m. In the Arndale Centre

'Thanks for coming with me, Jade,' said Holly. 'I need all the help I can get.'

'That's OK,' said Jade. 'I wanted to come – to get the latest Hot Totty CD. There's no chance of me being allowed to go to the concert, so that's the next best thing.'

'I wish the whole gang was coming,' sighed Holly. 'I mean, Cleo's still wittering on that her mum won't let her and Scott says it's too expensive. Andy's got tickets for him and Tansy, but now he's walking around with a face like a wet weekend, not talking about anything.'

Holly paused and examined a chocolate dinosaur.

'Four pounds ninety-nine! It's a rip off!' she exclaimed.

'So,' said Jade, 'you're going with Paul, I take it?

'Oh yes,' said Holly. 'There's only one tiny problem about it all.'

'What's that?'

'My parents don't know about it yet.'

4.20 p.m.

'That was inspired!' Holly clutched the paper bag to her chest. 'Thanks, Jade.'

She peered into the bag.

'I never knew you could buy single chocolates and get them iced,' she said.

'You did get eight, didn't you?' asked Jade.

'Yes,' beamed Holly. 'And if I lay them out in a line they spell "I LOVE YOU". He'll die!'

4.35 p.m. Surprise encounter

Jade had just waved goodbye to Holly and was crossing the park to Lime Avenue when she saw a familiar figure slouched on one of the benches by the miniature railway.

'Allegra! What are you doing here?'

Slowly Allegra raised her head and gave a lopsided grin.

'Hello,' she said.

'You've been crying! What's wrong?'

Allegra sniffed and wiped her nose with the back of her hand.

'Nothing,' she said. 'I'm fine.'

Jade took her hand.

'Listen,' she said firmly, 'you don't have to tell me what it is. You don't have to say a word. But don't try to pretend you're fine because you're not. You haven't been for days.'

Allegra looked at her for a long moment. And then she burst into tears.

'Oh Jade,' she said. 'I'm so miserable. I don't know what to do. I just want to die.'

5.00 p.m. Walking home

Jade handed her cousin another tissue.

'It'll be all right,' she said comfortingly.

'No, it won't. I can't do it any more. I don't want to do it. But I have to do it. And it's hopeless!'

Allegra gulped and wiped her eyes.

'But surely,' reasoned Jade patting her hand, 'if you tell Paula that acting's not your thing any more, she'll understand. It's not the end of the world.'

'You don't understand anything!' retorted Allegra angrily. 'You've only been here a few months.'

'So?'

'So you don't know how it's been,' sobbed

Allegra. 'Ever since I was little, I've danced and sang and been at stage school. Mum's convinced I'm going to make it big time. She's set her heart on it.'

'But that's because she thinks you enjoy it,' said Jade as they turned into Lime Avenue. 'I mean, to be honest, *I* thought you enjoyed it.'

Allegra shrugged.

'I used to,' she admitted. 'But now – I'm just a misfit. There's Candice, who's so sophisticated even though she's nearly a year younger than me, and Tamsin – well, she makes me look so gawky and stupid! This audition tomorrow will be hell. Hugo says . . .'

'What does Hugo say?'

'He says I need to get my act together, be more outrageous, develop attitude.'

Jade was about to say that she thought Allegra had attitude to spare, but thought that this was possibly not the best moment.

'And have you told him you hate the whole scene?' asked Jade.

'I can't do that!' gasped Allegra. 'He'd drop me just like that. He said he wants a girlfriend who's a star, someone really sassy!'

Jade pushed open the gate of their house and turned to face her cousin.

'Then he's not worth having,' she said firmly. 'Either he loves you for you, or he doesn't. You don't need him.'

Allegra's eyes narrowed and she glared at her cousin.

'Yes I do,' she shouted. 'I do need him. Who else have I got?'

She tossed her head and took a deep breath.

'And if you dare say a single word to my mother, I'll . . .'

Jade held up a hand.

'I won't,' she said. 'I promise. But Allegra, you have got someone, you know.'

'Oh yes? Like who?'

'Me,' said Jade.

6.30 p.m. Message of love

Holly slipped the long narrow box through Paul's letter box and smiled to herself.

It was just right. A secret sort of present delivered with no fuss. And with such a romantic message.

This time, no one would know. No one would care. And Paul was sure to be swept off his feet.

7.00 p.m. Question time

'I look good, yes?' José stood in front of the hall mirror, surveying his appearance.

'OK,' said Holly. 'Why are you taking Tansy out?'

José looked puzzled.

'Because she has said she will help with my project,' he said. 'It is of much importance to me to do well – and I am only here for six weeks.'

'Thank heavens for that,' said Holly.

Although I guess, she thought to herself, that as far as Andy is concerned, that will be five weeks and five days too long.

7.30 p.m. Head to head

'Angela?' Holly's father looked up as Holly pushed open the door of his study. 'Oh, it's you, Holly. Isn't your mother back yet?'

Holly shook her head.

'I've made spaghetti,' she said. 'Want some?'

'No thanks, I'm not hungry,' he said. 'But that was very thoughtful of you.'

Now! thought Holly. Go for it while he's in a good mood.

'Dad,' she said, perching on the edge of his desk. 'Could you possibly let me have an advance on my allowance?'

Her father raised an eyebrow.

'That's your mother's department,' he said.

'Yes, but she's so busy and I don't like to trouble her with trivia,' said Holly. 'And I really do need the money.'

'What for?'

How shall I put this? thought Holly.

'There's a concert I want to go to,' she said. 'And it's in aid of –'

'If you mean that appalling Rock thing, young lady, you can just forget it!' Her father pushed back his chair and stood up. 'Oh yes, I know all about it;

your mother told me you were angling to go. And the answer is categorically no!'

Holly jumped off the desk and wheeled round to face him.

'That is so unfair!' she stormed. 'All my friends are going – and what's more, Tansy's mum's going.'

'Oh well, that doesn't surprise me!' Her father gave a sarcastic laugh. 'That woman's nothing but an overgrown teenager herself. All those hippy clothes and incense smoking the house out.'

'I can't believe you said that!' shouted Holly. 'She's a really nice person – and a far fairer parent than you are!' She could feel her eyes swimming with tears. 'You are so stuffy! I didn't ask to be born as an afterthought, did I? I didn't ask to have a dad who was old enough to be my grandfather!'

Rupert slumped down in his chair again and brushed a hand across his brow.

'Holly, just go and get on with your homework or something, will you? I'm not feeling too hot and I don't need all this.'

'Oh, don't you?' shouted Holly. 'And I don't need you to tell me how to spend my life! And what's more, I'm not going to let you. I'm going to that concert, Dad, whether you like it or not.'

'You are most certainly not!' Rupert hauled himself to his feet. 'And if you speak to me – Aaaarh!'

Suddenly he doubled up, grabbing the corner of

the desk with one hand and clasping his chest with the other.

'Holly! Help . . . me!'

The words came out strangled and squeaky.

'Dad? Dad!'

Holly stood rooted to the spot as her father gasped, clutching at the air wildly and then, to her horror, fell in a crumpled heap on the floor. And lay completely still.

'DAD!' She dropped down on one knee beside him. 'Oh, help me! Somebody come and help me!'

She shook her father's shoulder. There was no response.

'Dad! Don't die, Dad! Dad, I'm sorry! Oh please, God, what should I do? Tell me what to do!

One minute later

'Ambulance, please, please, I need an ambulance!' Holly clutched the receiver until her knuckles were white. 'It's my dad. I think he's had a heart attack.'

She tried to calm herself.

'Address? Oh, yes. The Cedars, Weston Way. The house with the big trees at the front. My dad's name? Rupert Vine. He's sixty. Tell me what to do!'

After another long minute

'Loosen his tie, take off his belt, get a cushion to go under his knees.' Holly repeated the paramedic's instructions over and over to herself. 'Oh, Mum, where are you? Please, please come. I'm so scared.'

7.45 p.m. Rescued

'You did very well, young lady!' The paramedic patted Holly on the shoulder. 'Now don't you worry, your dad's in the best possible hands.'

At that moment, Holly heard the scrunch of gravel on the driveway followed by a car door slamming and the sound of feet pounding towards the front door.

'Holly! Rupert! Oh my God, what's happened?'

Holly flew to the door.

'Mum, oh, Mum, thank heavens you're back! I'm so sorry, Mum – I'm so, so sorry!'

7.50 p.m. Scared and lonely

Holly stood and watched as the ambulance disappeared down the drive and into the road. She had wanted to go too, but her mother had gently refused, telling her she must phone her brother and let José know what had happened when he got home.

'And you can't stay in the house alone with him,' her mother had fretted. 'It wouldn't be right.'

'But you'll be back, won't you?' Holly had asked. 'I mean, they'll make Dad better, won't they?'

There had been a slight pause, just too long for Holly to feel comfortable.

'I'll phone from the hospital,' Angela had said,

and Holly had seen tears in her eyes. 'Just pray, Holly. Keep praying for your dad.'

Now, turning back into the house, it was suddenly all too much. It was her fault. If she hadn't shouted at her father, told him he was too old to be a dad, been so horrid to him, he would never had had the heart attack.

She sank down in an armchair and began to cry. And once she had started, she couldn't stop.

8.00 p.m. In recovery mode

'You're not going out again, are you?' Jade eyed Allegra in surprise. 'You said you had to have an early night.'

'So I changed my mind,' said Allegra cheerfully, applying mascara in thick layers to her already-long eyelashes. 'I'm going to Mirage with Hugo and the crowd from school.'

Jade bit her tongue.

'You certainly seem more cheerful,' she ventured. 'What's changed?'

Allegra shrugged.

'It was just a passing mood,' she said. 'Chuck me that bottle of cola, will you? My throat's so sore.'

She took a big swig.

'It's all the singing that does it,' she said. 'Anyway, I must dash – catch you later, OK?'

Jade nodded.

'OK,' she said. 'Don't let Hugo or those others boss you about.'

Allegra tossed her head.

'He won't,' she assured her. 'I can handle the lot of them. Just watch me.'

8.15 p.m. More traumas

'Ring me, Mum, ring me.' Holly paced the sitting-room floor for the hundredth time. She had rung Richard but he was out, and her other brother Tom was abroad on business. She had tried watching TV, but she couldn't concentrate. She had tried to eat the spaghetti, but it was cold and congealed and, besides, she had lost her appetite. She just sat and flicked idly through a magazine, straining her ears for the phone.

The sound that made her jump was not the phone but the doorbell.

'She's back!' she thought joyously. She ran to the door and yanked it open.

'Holly, can I have a quick word?' It was Paul's mum and she was holding the precious box of chocolates.

'Well, I –'

'I found these addressed to Paul,' she said. 'With a note from you.'

Holly nodded. She wanted to say that Mrs Bennett had no right reading the note, but couldn't be bothered.

'Holly, these chocolates have got nuts in them,' she said.

'So?' said Holy dully. I want my mum.

101

'Paul is allergic to nuts,' she said. 'One bite of these and he would have been in hospital.'

Holly stared at her.

'No!' she said. 'No, I . . .' And burst into tears all over again.

8.30 p.m. Explanations

'Holly dear, I didn't mean you to get this upset!' Mrs Bennett fluttered over her. 'I only meant –'

'It's Dad,' said Holly. 'He's going to die and it's all my fault! I killed him. Just like I nearly killed Paul!'

8.45 p.m. Reassurance

'There!' Mrs Bennett put a tray of tea and a plate of shortbread on the coffee table. 'This will make you feel better.'

Holly tried to smile.

'Thank you,' she said. 'I'm sorry I made a fuss. I just feel so guilty.'

Mrs Bennett patted her hand.

'It's not your fault,' she said. 'Not about your dad, and not about Paul. People don't have heart attacks just because you shout at them, Holly.'

'Really?'

'Really,' said Mrs Bennett. 'He'd probably be working up to it for ages – stress, worry at work . . .'

Holly nodded.

'He resigned this week – only we weren't very kind about it.'

Mrs Bennett tactfully did not pursue the matter.

'As for Paul,' she said, 'you weren't to know that he has a nut allergy – and I shouldn't have sounded so cross. We mums worry, that's all. He should have told you.'

'He doesn't tell me much these days,' said Holly woefully. 'Perhaps I'm just not a very nice person.'

'Fiddlesticks!' retorted Mrs Bennett. 'Paul is just a typical boy. Words don't feature very much. Grunts he does awfully well.'

Despite her misery, Holly laughed.

'And what's all this about Saturday?' asked Mrs Bennett. 'The poem, you know.'

'Oh – you didn't see that, did you?'

Paul's mum nodded.

'Steve got hold of it and was teasing him,' she sighed. 'Saturday?'

'Oh,' sighed Holly. 'It was a pop concert. But I'm not allowed to go and anyway, it doesn't matter. Nothing matters now. Except Dad getting better. That's all I want.'

9.00 p.m. Discovery

Jade stretched, threw down her pen and slammed her Physics textbook shut. It was useless; she didn't understand it and she never would.

She rubbed her eyes wearily and idly stretched out a hand to pick up the cola bottle that Allegra had thrown on to the desk. Unscrewing the top, she took a big swig.

And spat it out in revulsion.

'What on earth?' She stared at the bottle, sniffed it, and then took another, far smaller, sip.

And then everything began to click into place – why Allegra was miserable one minute and as high as a kite the next, why she kept getting headaches in the middle of the night, and why Jade's precious suede desert boots were ruined.

This wasn't cola that Allegra was constantly swigging. Or at least, it was cola with something added.

And Jade was pretty sure it was alcohol.

Unless she was very much mistaken, Allegra was a secret drinker.

9.30 p.m. Together again

Holly threw herself into her mother's arms.

'You're back!' she cried. 'How's Dad?'

Angela rubbed a hand wearily across her eyes.

'They say he's managing to hold his own,' she said. 'That's good, isn't it, Holly? I mean, you do think that sounds hopeful, don't you?'

'Yes, definitely,' Holly had said firmly although her knees were shaking and she felt very sick. 'It's a good sign, I'm sure it is.'

'Oh, Holly . . .' Her mum's voice broke.

Holly wanted to cry too but she knew this wasn't the time.

'Come on, I've made you some sandwiches,' she said.

Angela shook her head.

'I can't eat,' she whispered.

'You must,' said Holly firmly. 'For my sake. For Dad's sake. Just do it.'

And for once, her mother did as she was told.

THURSDAY

8.00 a.m. Morning confrontations

'Good luck in the audition!' Jade hugged Allegra as she prepared to leave for school.

'Thanks,' said Allegra.

'I'll drive you to the station,' said Paula. 'I can drop Jade off on the way back.'

'Oh, if you must!' snapped Allegra. 'But don't get out of the car, all right?'

Paula sighed.

'If you say so,' she said.

'I do,' said Allegra.

8.30 a.m.

'Now here's your ticket, and there's ten pounds for expenses – oh and, darling, you have got your sheet music, haven't you?'

'YES!' Allegra was looking wild-eyed and flushed. 'Now just go, Mum, OK?'

'See you tonight, darling – with great news I hope.'

Jade waved out of the window as Paula manoeuvred the car into the stream of morning traffic. As they disappeared out of sight, Allegra still hadn't moved an inch.

8.35 a.m. Bad news

'Have you heard? Isn't it awful? Mr Boardman's going ape!'

Jade frowned as she passed the cluster of kids standing by the main door.

'What's up?' she asked.

'They've been again,' said Ella Hankinson.

'The vandals,' added Ursula Newley.

'What?' Scott gasped. 'Not more graffiti?'

Ella shook her head.

'Worse,' she said. 'They've trashed the float. It's a total write-off.'

8.45 a.m.

'I don't believe it,' Scott said for the fourth time. The float lorry was standing, a burnt-out shell, at the back of the Art Block. Not a trace of the mountain was left – just a pile of charred remains and a slashed tarpaulin.

And scrawled across the cab of the lorry in bright orange paint were the words 'Poxy West Green'.

'Who do you think did it?' asked Cleo.

'Some mindless jerk, I guess.' Andy looked disgusted. 'My dad will go ballistic.'

'All that work on the float for nothing,' sighed Jade.

'No,' sighed Cleo. 'Now we've got nothing to look forward to on Saturday.'

'Oh get real!' cried Tansy. 'We've still got Rock-It. I can't see why you don't all come with me. My mum's up for it.'

'Your mum!' the others chorused.

'You're not going to be there with your *mum*, surely?' interjected Cleo.

'No,' said Tansy patiently. 'I am not going to *be* there with my mum; I'm just using her to *get* me there. She'd be a very good alibi with the parents.' .

'I'm up for it,' said Scott. 'My gran sent me twenty pounds yesterday.'

'Really?' Jade looked amazed. 'Well, I suppose I could get the money from my building society – as long as my aunt doesn't find out.'

'Oh, little Miss Moneybags,' said Andy.

Jade bit her lip.

'It's my inheritance money – from when my mum and dad died.'

Andy's face fell.

'Oh, Jade, I'm sorry – I didn't mean it. I'm kind of jangly right now.'

Jade smiled and nodded.

'I know Holly wants to go,' said Cleo. 'Where is she?'

'Haven't you heard?' Tansy exclaimed. 'Her dad had a heart attack last night – he's in hospital, really sick. I don't somehow think Holly will be thinking about pageants or concerts or anything else right now.'

9.05 a.m. In Assembly

'And so,' sighed Mr Boardman, rocking on his heels, 'because of the behaviour of some mindless vandals, West Green will no longer have a float at the Town Pageant.'

The room broke out in an uproar.

'But,' said Mr Boardman, holding up a hand, 'I expect every one of you to rally round, dress up and take your collecting buckets on to the streets on Saturday. We can still have a fun day despite this disappointment.'

'You bet we can,' murmured Tansy. 'More than you'll ever know.'

9.30 a.m. Sick visiting

'Thank heavens for Clarity!' sighed Mrs Vine as she and Holly drove to the hospital. 'If she hadn't offered to take José, I don't know what I would have done. I hope Tansy won't mind being turned out of her room.'

'She won't, Mum,' said Holly. 'She'll be over the moon.'

10.00 a.m. Too much

Holly held tightly on to her mum's hand as they walked together into the Coronary Care Unit. Richard, Holly's brother, had spent the night at the hospital and had left for work, promising to be back the next day.

'He's a bit better this morning,' the nurse told them. 'But he's still heavily sedated.'

Holly moved closer to the bed and gulped. It didn't look like her dad. His face was grey, and there was a tube coming out of his mouth and another from his nose. A machine at the side of his bed was bleeping steadily and fluid was dripping through a clear plastic tube into a syringe stuck in his arm.

Suddenly Holly felt sick and light-headed. The floor of the room began swirling like a carousel and the drumming in her ears got louder and louder.

'Holly?' She heard her mother's voice from a long way off. And then everything went black.

10.10 a.m. More confessions

'It's all right, darling. Just keep sipping the water.' Holly's mum was holding her hand tightly. 'You're going to be fine.'

'Mum,' whispered Holly. 'I've got something to tell you.'

'What's that, darling?'

Holly swallowed and tried to keep her voice even.

'It's all my fault,' she said. 'It's my fault Dad had that heart attack. And if he dies . . .'

'HOLLY! Don't even think it!' Her mother cried. 'Dad won't die, he can't die, he . . .'

Her voice faltered and she pulled herself together.

'And of course it wasn't your fault,' she said. 'How could it have been?'

Holly sniffed.

'We had a row,' she gulped. 'I wanted to go to Rock-It, and he said no, and I said he was stuffy and old and then he kind of cried out and fell down and . . .'

Her mother opened her arms and enveloped her in a big hug.

'Darling,' she said, 'I promise you, faithfully, it was not your fault.' She emphasized each word carefully. 'Do you understand me?'

'How do you know?'

'Because,' said her mum softly, biting her lip and blinking rather rapidly, 'I have a horrible feeling that it was mine.'

10.50 a.m. Further confessions

Holly and her mum were sitting in the hospital cafeteria, sipping tea and sharing a ham and tomato roll. Half an hour before, Rupert had opened his eyes, smiled and fallen asleep again. It wasn't much, but the nurse said they should take heart from that and go and have some lunch.

'I blame myself,' said Angela for the fifth time. 'He said his arm hurt – remember? – and I said he was making a fuss about nothing.'

'What's his arm got to do with his heart attack?' asked Holly.

'The doctor said it was a warning sign,' said her mother, blinking back tears. 'And I was too wrapped up in my own life to take any notice. And for that, I will never forgive myself.'

She sipped her tea.

'I've known for ages that Dad was fed up at the university,' said Angela. 'I blame myself for not listening more. I was just so scared, you see.'

'Scared?' asked Holly.

Her mother nodded.

'Dad was on a good salary and his job was secure. The thought of him doing something that paid less terrified me.'

She sipped her tea.

'Now I don't care if we live on a pittance, as long as he gets well,' she said. 'I need him so badly – I can't do anything without him.'

Holly frowned.

'You do everything,' she pointed out. 'Shopping, cooking, cleaning, charity work . . .'

Her mum nodded.

'But I can only do it because he's there in the background, like a rock,' she said. 'You'll understand one day. When you have someone you really need, someone you lean on.'

Holly sighed.

'Sometimes I don't think I will ever find anyone just for me,' she said. 'I don't think I'm a very lovable person.'

Her mum took her hand and squeezed it.

'Well, I do,' she said. 'Very lovable indeed.'

2.45 p.m. Soul searching

'Jade Williams! Nobody else seems to find my lesson so boring that they have to yawn repeatedly.' Miss Partridge glared across the room.

'Sorry,' said Jade. It's all very well for you, she thought, you weren't kept awake half the night while Allegra tossed and turned and complained of feeling sick again. Of course, now she knew why her cousin was in such a state, and she also knew she had to do something about it. But what?

If she told Paula, Allegra would never forgive her. And if she didn't tell Paula, and something awful happened, Jade would be the one to get the blame.

Maybe she would just wait and see what happened. After all, it wasn't as if Allegra had ever been caught drinking before. And maybe it was just the pressure of this audition.

I'll wait till tonight and have it out with Legs myself, she thought. In the meantime, I need to tackle Paula about something completely different.

4.30 p.m. Looking over her shoulder

'Dad? It's me, Cleo. Fine, thanks. How's Fleur?
Good. Look, I need a favour.'

She held her breath and crossed her fingers
behind her back.

'Could you lend me fifteen pounds? I'd pay it
back. It's for . . . a music festival.' She thought that
sounded more parental than a pop concert.

'You will! Wow, thanks, Dad! And you'll mail it
right away? You're a star. Roy? No, I asked, but he
couldn't. I know, Dad. I know you're a much more
generous man than he is. Thanks, Dad. Love you
lots. Bye!'

Now, she thought, replacing the receiver softly,
all I need is the excuse. Which could prove a lot
harder than raising the funds.

5.00 p.m. More clock watching

'She should be back soon,' fretted Paula, looking at
the clock. 'I do hope it's gone well. I really thought
she would ring.'

'Maybe she wanted to surprise you,' suggested
Joshua, looking up from *Insect World*.

I guess, thought Jade, Allegra's about to surprise
you a lot more than you bargained for.

'Paula,' she said, adopting as casual a voice as
she could manage, 'have you seen this?' She
pointed to the evening paper.

'What, dear?'

'There's a rock concert on Saturday at The

Bowl. I've never been to one before.'

'And you won't ever be going to one while I have charge of you,' declared Paula. 'So don't even think about it.'

That's that then, thought Jade. Unless . . .

Slowly a smile drifted across her lips. There was a way. And it might just work.

6.30 p.m. Schemes

'Do you think it will work?' Jade whispered to Tansy down the phone. 'Are you sure? Good. Well, you do your stuff your end, and I'll sort things over here. Thanks, Tansy, you're a mate.'

7.30 p.m. Panic stations

'That's it!' cried Paula. 'She's two hours late – I'm phoning Candice's mother to see what's happening. Jade, start the washing up.'

'Please,' muttered Jade.

7.35 p.m. A moment of truth

'Oh my God!' Jade could hear her aunt's voice rising in panic. 'What do you mean, she wasn't on the train? I took her to the station myself. Not at the audition?'

Jade pressed her ear closer to the door.

'Yes, yes I will. The police. Yes. Oh dear God.'

Jade jumped back at the sound of Paula's footsteps approaching the door.

'Allegra never went! She wasn't on the train! Something's happened, I know it has. She's been abducted, she's ill, she's –'

'Hang on,' said Jade calmly. 'Maybe she just changed her mind.'

'Oh, for heaven's sake, Jade, if you haven't got anything sensible to say, keep your mouth shut! Allegra's been living for this audition, the stage is her life –'

'NO IT'S NOT!' The words were out before Jade had considered them. 'She's fed up with it, she told me so. She's miserable and what's more –'

'Jade! How can you say such a thing?' Paula stared at her in disbelief. 'I know you've always been jealous of poor Legs –'

'I have not!' stormed Jade.

'. . . But all she's ever wanted is to be an actress.'

'No,' said Jade. 'That's all *you* ever wanted. It's not what she wanted at all.'

She took her aunt's arm.

'Before you phone the police,' she said, 'I think there is something I should tell you.'

8.25 p.m. The prodigal returns

Jade couldn't concentrate on homework. Maybe she should have told Paula about the drinking as well. What if Allegra had passed out somewhere? She would wait five more minutes and then she'd tell her.

They'd agreed to wait until 8.30. It was almost that now.

Suddenly the doorbell rang. Jade jumped up and rushed downstairs.

'Allegra! Darling! Thank God!'

'Legs!' Jade was just in time to see Allegra push her mother out of the way, clamp her hand over her mouth and rush to the kitchen sink.

Where she was horribly and very noisily sick.

8.30 p.m. Joy

'I think we had better go home, darling,' said Mrs Vine, squeezing Holly's hand.

'We can't leave him!' Holly protested. 'What if he wakes up?'

'I'm here,' said Richard, her older brother. 'He's not alone.'

Holly leaned over and kissed her father's forehead.

'I love you, Dad,' she said. 'Really I do.'

She turned to go.

'Holly, wait!' her brother called urgently. 'Look.'

Rupert Vine opened his eyes.

'Love you too, Hollyberry,' he said.

Holly's eyes filled with tears. He hadn't called her that since she was tiny.

Angela gasped with delight. Richard grinned.

'He's going to make it, isn't he, Mum?' Holly whispered.

Thursday

From the pillow there was the slightest move-
ment.

'You bet I am,' her father murmured.

FRIDAY

7.30 a.m. Handing out instructions

Tansy poured herself some juice and turned to her mother.

'Now you have got that, haven't you?' she said. 'You know what you have to do.'

Clarity nodded obediently.

'Yes, dear,' she said. 'I have it off by heart.'

'Good,' said Tansy. 'Don't get it wrong.'

7.45 a.m. Taking on Allegra

'Allegra,' said Jade.

'Go away,' said Allegra. 'Can't you see I'm dying?'

'We've done this bit before,' said Jade firmly. 'And I know why you feel so ill.'

Allegra propped herself up on one arm and eyed her cousin suspiciously.

'What do you mean? It's this bug – I can't get

119

rid of it.'

Jade opened a drawer.

'You mean it's the contents of this bottle,' she retorted. 'Legs, you're a fool.'

She waited for the outburst, to be told she was an interfering cow and that she should go and boil her head.

'You haven't told Mum?' Allegra gasped.

'Not yet,' said Jade. 'But unless you promise never to do it again – well, not till you're old enough anyway – I shall tell her.

'I won't do it,' Allegra said. 'I don't need to now, do I? I got out of the audition and, thanks to you, Mum's promised to talk things over.'

She went to stand up, groaned and sank back on the bed.

'Thanks, Jade,' she said.

'And you won't drink again?' said Jade.

'No,' said Allegra firmly. 'I promise.'

8.00 a.m. The end of all my hopes, the end of all my dreams

'Coming, José?' Tansy held open the front door of the cottage.

'I will walk with you to the corner,' he said, picking up his folder. 'There I meet my friend.'

Tansy looked aggrieved.

'What friend?'

'She is from my college,' he said.

'She?'

Tansy looked more aggrieved. José nodded happily.

'She is called Concepta,' he said. 'She is very beautiful.'

I hate her already, thought Tansy.

'Tomorrow you will meet her,' he added. 'I take her to the popping concert. It is good for her.'

'Never mind her!' Tansy burst out. 'You said you were going with me.'

José looked up in astonishment.

'But now you go with your mother, and the other children,' he said. 'This is so, yes?'

'No! Yes! I mean, she's taking us and we're not children – I thought you wanted to go to be with me.'

He laughed.

'I like you, Tansy,' he said. 'You are fun. But now I have a girlfriend, and I wish spend the time with her.'

He paused and eyed her gently.

'You will like her,' he said.

'Frankly,' said Tansy, 'I very much doubt it.'

8.15 a.m. Rejection

She was stomping up the hill when Andy caught up with her.

'You look as fed up as I feel,' he said. 'What's wrong?'

'Go away!' snapped Tansy. 'Just go and be miserable somewhere else.'

'I need to talk,' he said.

'Well, find someone else,' said Tansy. 'I want to be alone.'

9.00 a.m. Setting the scene

'Hello, Paula? Clarity Meadows here. Look, Tansy's having a little sleepover on Saturday night – to make up for the disappointment about the float. She'd love Jade to come . . . To sleep, yes . . . Paula, are you all right? . . . Oh good . . . She can? Terrific . . . Oh, don't you worry, she'll be fine . . . A video? Oh yes, yes, great idea. See her then! Ciao!'

One down, two to go, she thought, ticking off the list that her daughter had given her.

Cleo was next . . .

11.30 a.m. Heart to heart

Holly slammed the receiver down on the school pay phone. Out of order again and just when she wanted to phone the hospital. Her mum had said that school was the best place for her now that her dad was getting better, but she didn't want to be there. She wanted to be with her father. You heard about people who looked as if they were recovering and then suddenly got worse. What if no one told her? What if he asked for her and she wasn't there?

'Oh, Dad!' She didn't realize she had said the words out loud until Andy Richards touched her arm.

122

'Are you OK?' he asked. 'Sorry to hear about your father – Tansy told me.'

Holly smiled.

'Thanks,' she said. 'It's just so awful, knowing he's ill and not being able to do anything.'

'Tell me about it,' said Andy. 'That's how I feel about my mum.'

Holly saw him blink furiously.

'I didn't know she was ill,' she said gently. 'Tansy never said.'

'Tansy,' said Andy miserably, 'doesn't seem to care. I tried telling her but . . .'

'So tell me,' said Holly hastily, in case he asked just why Tansy was being so off with him.

Andy bit his lip.

'She keeps throwing up all the time, falling asleep at the table, not eating . . .'

Holly stared at him.

'And my dad's being weird too,' he said. 'One minute he's shouting at her that it's all her fault and she can't expect to swan off for months on end and then come home and expect him to pick up the pieces.'

He gulped.

'And then – then he's hugging her and saying everything will be fine and the doctors can sort it.'

'Oh,' said Holly thoughtfully.

'Do you think she's got something really serious?' Andy asked.

Holly was about to say something and then changed her mind.

'I guess it's just a bug,' she said. 'Try not to worry.

12.00 p.m. More soul searching

Jade chewed the end of her pen. Allegra would stop drinking now, wouldn't she? After all, she had promised. And she was going to talk to Paula about giving up acting. There was no need for Jade to drop her in it. Not just as they seemed to be getting on a bit better. It would all be fine now.

12.15 p.m.

Holly couldn't bear it any longer. She would go in the lunch hour. If she ran she could just make it. And if she wasn't back in time, that would be just too bad.

12.45 p.m. Bedside manners

'Holly, you shouldn't have come. You should be at school concentrating on your work.'

Holly burst into tears.

'Darling, I didn't mean to nag . . .'

'It's OK, Dad,' she sobbed. 'I've never been so happy to hear you nagging in my entire life.'

12.50 p.m.

'I think Mr Vine should rest now.' The nurse came and touched Holly on the shoulder. 'Your mother's waiting in the corridor.'

'Just one minute,' pleaded her father. 'There's something I have to sort out with my daughter.'

'Only one,' said the nurse, retreating behind the screens.

'Holly, will you do something for me?'

'Anything, Dad. Anything at all.'

Her father eased himself up on the pillows and took something from the bedside locker.

'Take this and go to the rock concert,' he said.

Holly gasped. He had handed her three ten-pound notes.

'No, Dad,' she cried. 'I know you don't like those things and I didn't mean to cause trouble and –'

'Holly,' her dad said. 'I was grouchy. I felt ill and old and scared. I want you to go. I want you to live life to the full. While you have the chance.'

She stared him.

'Oh, Dad,' she said. 'Thank you.'

'But, darling,' he said as she stood up to kiss him. 'You will take care, won't you? I love you so.'

'I love you too, Dad,' she said. 'And I promise nothing will go wrong. Nothing at all.'

1.15 p.m. Something to think about
'I'll drive you back, sweetheart,' said Holly's mother, as they crossed the hospital quadrangle. 'And then I'll stop off and get your tickets.'

'Thanks, Mum,' said Holly, squeezing her hand. 'You're sure . . .?'

'Certain,' smiled Angela. 'Come on.'

'Hang on, Mum!' Holly stopped dead in her tracks. 'That's Andy's mum – I recognize her from junior school.'

'Really, dear? Now do come on.'

'Look where she's going,' said Holly.

Mrs Vine looked.

'Antenatal and Maternity,' she read. 'Visiting someone, I imagine.'

I don't think so, thought Holly with a shock. I think Mrs Richards is pregnant. And Andy doesn't have a clue.

3.00 p.m. A change of mind

'And so I can go!' Holly beamed at Tansy.

'Ace!' said Tansy. 'Let's hope Paul's still free.'

'I'm not asking him,' said Holly.

'What?' Tansy exploded. 'After all I've been through with you . . .'

'I've kind of messed up there,' admitted Holly. 'Yet again. And I just don't dare make things worse.'

4.00 p.m. A little adult intervention

'Mrs Bennett? Clarity Meadows here. We met at the Vines' cheese and wine . . . that's it, I'm the gardening lady . . . Yes, so sad about Rupert, but I hear he's doing well . . . Holly? Well, actually, it's about Holly that I wanted a word.'

Clarity took a deep breath.

'Now look, before I start, all this is Tansy's idea . . .'

6.00 p.m. *More parental surprises*

'Can I come in, darling?' Diana knocked on Cleo's bedroom door.

'I don't suppose you are any good at biology, are you?' sighed Cleo.

'Useless, absolutely useless,' said Diana cheerfully. 'I just popped up to say it's fine for Saturday.'

'*What?*' Cleo gasped. 'You mean you'll actually let me go to –'

'Tansy's sleepover party? Of course, poppet! Might they like to see the video of me in *Iolanthe*, do you think? No? Must fly. Drinks party with my agent. Such fun!'

And with that she was gone, leaving behind her a cloud of *Allure* and a daughter with a very broad grin on her face.

8.15 p.m. *A new dimension*

Holly ran downstairs and answered the door.

'Hi,' said Paul. 'Can I come in?'

Holly took a deep breath.

'Look, I'm really sorry about the chocolate – I didn't know you were allergic, and I'm sorry about the dumb poem and everything. And if you've come to give me a hard time –'

'Hang on,' Paul laughed. 'Can't a guy get inside the door?'

She stepped back and let him pass.

'I came,' he said, 'to say I was sorry about your dad – and to ask what time you want me to pick you up on Saturday.'

Holly's eyes widened.

'What?' she squeaked.

'Unless, of course, you're taking someone else to Rock-It.'

'Paul!' she gasped and flung her arms round his neck. He stiffened.

'Sorry,' she said, pulling back and feeling the disappointment wash over her. 'That's really kind of you. But you don't have to do it. I know that you don't really want to be with me.'

'But I do!' Paul asserted. 'That's the whole point. Like I said to Tansy –'

'Tansy? What's she got to do with this?'

Paul looked sheepish.

'She came over,' he lied quickly, 'to tell me about your dad. And . . . I asked about Rock-It and she said she thought you'd let me use your other ticket.'

'I'll kill her,' snarled Holly.

'Don't!' laughed Paul. 'I really do want to go with you. I want to do loads of things with you. The thing is, I just don't want' – his face coloured – 'the rest of it,' he finished lamely.

Holly stared at him.

'I like you, Holly. A lot. More than any other girl I know. But I just don't know about . . . well,

getting serious and everything. All these pre-
sents . . .'

Holly thought fast. He definitely liked her. But it
wasn't the big love thing and she was going to lose
him. Unless . . .

'It's OK,' she said, suddenly feeling very mature
and strong. 'We can skip the other stuff.'

'Really? You'll come, then? Without wanting . . .'

'Without wanting to get serious or anything,' she
lied.

SATURDAY

12.30 p.m. A little white lie

'Jade, dear?' Paula looked up from her newspaper. 'Why are you taking a bucket and a bin bag to a sleepover party?'

Jade thought fast. She could hardly tell her aunt that you needed a bucket to stand on in order to see the stage.

'We're still going collecting at the Pageant,' she said hastily. 'The bucket's for the money and the bin bag . . . is to sit on if the ground's wet.'

Well, at least that bit's true, she thought.

'So did you talk to Allegra?' Jade asked. 'I mean, about her giving up acting?'

Paula nodded.

'Yes, dear, and it's all fine.'

'Oh good,' sighed Jade. 'I'm sure she was very grateful.'

'Oh yes,' said Paula. 'I made her see sense.'

'*What?*'

'I told her that once she's over this bug, she'll see things in a different light,' said Paula. 'She's just very run down, that's all. Now off you go, and have a great time.'

I don't think, thought Jade miserably, that I handled that very well. Not very well at all.

4.00 p.m.

'I go now, Mrs Meadows,' José said, gathering up a coat and scarf that would not have looked out of place on the catwalk. 'I must not keep Concepta waiting.'

Tansy swallowed and tried to look uninterested.

'I'm sorry I can't fit you into the van, José,' said Clarity.

'Oh, don't worry,' he said. 'We like to be alone.'

'Well, you're going to the wrong place then, aren't you?' said Tansy.

4.15 p.m.

'Right, girls, let's hit the road!' Clarity clattered down the uncarpeted stairs of the cottage and grabbed her car keys from the hall table.

'MUM! What have you got on?' Tansy gazed at her mother open-mouthed.

'Aren't they great?' she cooed. 'Loon pants – I haven't worn them since nineteen seventy-three and they still fit.'

'They're ... different, aren't they?' ventured Cleo.

'My mother's different,' muttered Tansy wryly. 'Come on – before she digs out her rope sandals.'

Jade giggled.

'Now there's a thought,' murmured Clarity.

'Mum. Car. Now.'

5.45 p.m.

'Oh, isn't this just so exciting?' Clarity manoeuvred her new minivan into the car park. 'The lights, the noise, the crowds – it reminds me of Glastonbury.'

She looked whimsically across the vast Bowl into which the crowds were steadily pouring.

'I was really rebellious when I was young, Jade,' she began. 'Foot loose and fancy free . . .'

'MUM!' Tansy interjected. 'Just go now, will you? We've got to meet up with Holly and the others.'

'All right, darling,' said Clarity. 'I'll go and find Henry. Now look, I will meet you by Gate C at exactly eleven o'clock. Understood?'

'But it doesn't end till midnight,' protested Tansy.

'Eleven,' said her mother. 'That's quite late enough.'

'Whatever happened to rebellious?' said Tansy.

6.30 p.m. Claiming their pitch.

'I can't believe we're here!' Cleo breathed. 'Look at it.'

The sea of people stretched from the edge of the

huge Bowl to the stage. Vast screens surrounded the area and amplifiers were already booming out the sounds of the first warm-up band.

'Now,' said Tansy, 'you spread out your bin bags like this. And then line up the buckets and stand on them. See?'

'Great!' enthused Jade, standing on one and peering over the heads of the crowds in front.

'And then you need a marker,' ordered Tansy.

'What for?'

'So that we know where to come back to if we get separated,' sighed Tansy.

'How come you know so much?' asked Cleo.

'I'm very well read,' said Tansy.

7.45 p.m.

'I'm getting on the last bus away from you, the last bus away . . .'

'This is brilliant!' enthused Paul, handing Holly a chocolate bar. 'I never realized it would be so big.'

'How come you know the words?' asked Holly. 'I didn't know you were into Hot Totty.'

'There's a lot you don't know about me,' said Paul. 'Come to think of it, there's a lot I don't know about me.'

That's what I like about him, thought Holly dreamily. He's so deep.

8.00 p.m. Damping down
'It's starting to rain,' said Cleo anxiously. 'We'll get wet.'

'Who cares?' cried Tansy. 'Have a sandwich.'

8.04 p.m.
'Actually,' said Holly, 'it's raining quite hard. Did anyone bring an umbrella?'

'Dead uncool,' said Tansy. 'Where's the Pepsi?'

8.05 p.m.
'Put the bin bags on your head,' suggested Jade as the rain pelted down.

'Now I've got mud on my hair,' moaned Holly.

8.45 p.m.
'Come on, Andy, rock!' Tansy grabbed his arm and began swaying to the beat of Hot Totty.

Andy stood rigid and unsmiling, his collar turned up against the rain.

'Hey, loosen up, Andy! This is such a funky sound! What's the matter with you?'

Andy turned and stared at her.

'What,' he said, 'do you care?'

9.10 p.m. Rather more bother than before
'Waaa! Brilliant!'

Jade was clapping so hard that she nearly fell off her bucket.

'I've never had such a great time,' she said to

Scott as a great roar swept through The Bowl. 'Hey look, it's Shiny Vinyl!'

The crowd started surging forward, eager to get as close as possible to the main band of the evening.

'Link arms!' ordered Holly.

She grabbed hold of Paul, ecstatic at having an excuse to get closer to him. The others all seized hold of one another and began slithering down the slope. The rain was beating down relentlessly by now and the ground was getting slippery.

Suddenly a huge group of screaming kids lurched down the bank behind them, pushing them forward so suddenly that it took all their effort to remain upright.

'Great, isn't it?' shouted Holly rather nervously.

'Mmm,' muttered Cleo.

'Mega,' said Tansy.

And fell face first into the mud.

9.15 p.m. *Even more bother than before*

Jade wasn't sure how she got separated from the rest of the gang, but suddenly she was surrounded by a sea of faces she didn't recognize.

'Scott!' she called in panic and began pushing her way back up the hill.

Suddenly she caught sight of an ambulance weaving its way cautiously along the top of the bank, and a crowd of people clustering round a figure lying prone on the grass.

'Scott!' She scrambled, slipping and sliding to the top. 'Oh no! Please, no!'

She stared at the huddled shape being coaxed awake by the paramedics. It wasn't, as she had feared for one moment, Scott.

It was Allegra.

9.16 p.m. Serious bother

'Hugo, what's happened? What's wrong with Allegra?'

Hugo shrugged.

'Can't hold her drink,' he said.

'You let her *drink*?' Jade shouted. 'How could you . . .?'

She wheeled round as someone tapped her on the shoulder.

'Jade, thank goodness – I couldn't find you.' It was Scott, breathless and looking wild-eyed. 'Something's happened.'

'Too right,' said Jade. 'Hang on.'

She grabbed the arm of the paramedic.

'That's my cousin and she's drunk!' she cried.

'We guessed,' said the ambulance man. 'Are you with her?'

'I wasn't,' said Jade. 'But I am now. I'm coming with her.'

They lifted her gently onto the stretcher.

'I'll come with you,' offered Scott.

Jade shook her head.

'No – you have to find a phone and ring Paula,'

she said. 'Tell her to come to the hospital.'

Scott nodded.

'Only there's a problem,' he said.

'What?' Jade sounded irritated.

'She doesn't know you're here, does she?' he reasoned. 'She thinks you're watching a video at Tansy's house.'

Jade swallowed.

'I'll just have to worry about that later,' she said. 'Right now, Allegra's sick – and it's all my fault.'

9.45 p.m. Enough is enough

'Tansy,' said Andy, as the bands changed over. 'I'm sorry I snapped. I need to talk.'

'No you don't!' cried Tansy. 'Here come Man Overboard. You need to rave!'

She grabbed his arm. He shook her off.

'I've had enough,' he said suddenly. 'I'm going.'

9.46 p.m. A listening ear

'Andy, wait!' Holly pushed and shoved through the jostling crowds and grabbed Andy's arm. 'Don't go!'

'Why not?' he said. 'I can't enjoy all this. I'm just so worried about my mum.'

'What's the problem?' asked Holly.

'She was so sick today she passed out. I think she's got . . .'

'What?'

'I think she's got cancer, Holly. I think she's come home to die.'

He pulled away.

'I'm going now,' he said. 'I want to get home.'

10.00 p.m.

'Is Andy OK?' Paul asked as Holly slithered back to him.

'No,' said Holly. 'I wish I knew what to say.'

'Sometimes saying nothing is best,' said Paul.

I've never had a philosophical boyfriend before, thought Holly. It's so uplifting.

10.05 p.m. Home truths

'I just don't believe it!' Tansy wailed to Holly yet again. 'I come out with a guy and he goes and abandons me.'

'You can hardly be surprised,' said Holly.

'I couldn't help falling over and ruining my clothes,' she said.

'I don't mean that,' retorted Holly, raising her voice over the music. 'Andy wouldn't care what you looked like. You don't deserve him, you know.'

'What do you mean?' demanded Tansy, abandoning her attempt to join in a Mexican wave.

'Well, all week he's been worried sick about his mum and trying to talk to you and all you've thought about is José.'

Tansy swallowed.

'And he bought you tickets for this gig and what did you do? Treat him like he didn't matter.'

Tansy swallowed again and nibbled a fingernail.

'OK, so maybe I was a bit off,' she said. 'But all relationships come to an end some time.'

Holly glared at her.

'Oh, great!' she said. 'So you just drop a guy when he's down, is that it? Tansy, he thinks his mum is seriously ill. He thinks she's got cancer.'

Tansy looked shocked.

'Oh no! Really? I thought . . . well, I don't know what I thought really, but . . . that's awful!'

'You could make it up to him,' said Holly.

'How?'

'By thinking of a kind way to tell him the truth.'

'What do you mean? That his mum is going to die?'

Holly shook her head.

'She's not ill,' she said. 'I'm almost sure she's pregnant. I saw her going into the Antenatal Department when I was visiting Dad.'

Tansy looked gobsmacked.

'But they're old!' she cried. 'Still, I guess Andy will be relieved. Maybe that's why his dad was in a mood when . . . Oh!'

'Precisely,' said Holly. 'Mrs Richards has been away from home for eight months. It's hardly likely that Andy's dad is the father, is it?'

10.30 p.m.

'Man Overboard aren't as good as the rest, are they?' said Holly.

'No,' agreed Tansy.

'I think,' said Cleo, 'it's because we're sort of . . . well . . .'

'Ready to go home?' said Holly.

No one dared be the first to agree.

'Scott!' Cleo looked up and beamed with relief. 'Where's Jade?'

'Gone to hospital,' he said.

'*What?*'

'Oh, not her,' he added hastily. 'With Allegra. Her cousin. She's sick.'

He sank down on the wet grass.

'I had to phone Allegra's mum. She's not a happy woman.'

Tansy raised her eyebrows.

'Well, of course she's not if Allegra's sick,' she reasoned.

'It's not just that,' said Scott. 'She didn't know Jade was coming here. And she's out for your mum's blood.'

'Ah,' said Tansy. 'Whoops!'

10.50 p.m. Mother on the loose

'We'd better head for the gate,' sighed Tansy. 'Mum will be waiting and we need to warn her.'

'She won't,' said Holly. 'Look.'

She pointed up to the giant screen that was

showing pictures of the crowd as the bands changed places.

'Oh no!'

There, in brilliant close-up for all the world to see, was Clarity Meadows in a clinch with an ancient, bald-headed guy wearing a purple bandanna round his head and an earring that would have been more at home on Captain Hook.

'I think,' sighed Tansy, 'she's just entering another rebellious phase.'

11.30 p.m. In the Casualty Department

'How could you do this, Jade? First you go to this rock concert behind my back and then you let Allegra get into this state!'

Paula was pacing the floor of the Casualty Department waiting room, wringing her hands in despair.

'Don't blame me!' shouted Jade. 'OK, so I should've told you about the concert, but I didn't know Legs was going – and I didn't make her drink. Hugo did.'

Paula's eyes widened.

'Hugo? He was there? Why didn't he come in the ambulance with her?'

'Because he's a jerk who thinks of no one but himself,' retorted Jade. 'I'm sorry, Paula, really I am – I just didn't think Allegra would drink again, not after . . .'

She paused, knowing she had said too much.

'Again?' gasped Paula. 'You mean – this isn't the first time?'

Jade shook her head miserably.

'That bug she had,' she said. 'It wasn't a bug. Allegra's been topping up her coke bottle with alcohol.'

'And you knew?' Paula's voice was icy cold.

Jade nodded miserably.

'She promised she would stop,' she said. 'And I thought –'

'No, you didn't, Jade,' said Paula. 'You didn't think at all.'

SUNDAY

*Midnight. In the kitchen of 3 Plough
Cottages, feeling flat*

'Mrs Meadows?' Cleo asked Clarity nervously as
they sipped hot chocolate before going to bed. 'Do
you think Jade's aunt will tell my mum that we
went to the concert?'

Clarity sighed.

'Undoubtedly,' she said. 'Judging by that phone
call just now, Paula thinks I'm the scum of the
earth.'

Tansy patted Cleo's hand.

'Don't worry,' she said. 'Your mum won't throw
a whoopsie. She's cool.'

'My stepdad isn't,' sighed Cleo. 'And I don't
reckon my dad will be too chuffed about it either.
That's the worst thing about parents getting
divorced.'

'What is?' asked Clarity.

'You get double punishments when things go wrong.'

12.10 a.m. Discharged!

'You can take Allegra home now, Mrs Webb.' The doctor peered at Paula over his spectacles. 'And may I suggest that you have a long and serious talk with your daughter about the perils of alcohol. Perhaps some counselling . . .'

'Counselling?' Paula exclaimed. 'Allegra doesn't need counselling. We're not some dysfunctional family – we're happy, united and –'

'Mrs Webb,' said the doctor patiently, 'people who are feeling happy and valued and at peace with their world do not drink themselves into oblivion. And particularly not at fifteen years of age. Talk to her, Mrs Webb. And do please listen.'

Paula swallowed.

'I will, doctor,' she said. 'Thank you.'

Jade hugged Allegra.

'Don't you ever dare give me a fright like that again!' she said.

'Sorry,' muttered Allegra. 'I've been a total idiot, haven't I?'

'Yes,' said Jade cheerfully. 'Join the club.'

12.15 a.m. Lovelorn from Madrid

Tansy, Cleo and Mrs Meadows were just going upstairs to bed when the front door slammed.

'Oh José, you're back. Good evening?'

José flung his jacket on the floor.

'No. Not good evening. Not at all.'

'Oh dear,' said Clarity. 'What went wrong?'

José closed his eyes and held his hands to his head.

'I cannot speak of it,' he said. 'I am a broken man.'

'Oh, right,' said Clarity. 'I won't pry then.'

José looked alarmed.

'Oh, but I will tell you,' he said. 'Concepta has lied to me, cheated me, deceived me. How can this be that a woman would treat me so?'

Tansy winked at Cleo, who made a desperate effort not to laugh.

'What happened?' asked Clarity.

'Tonight, in middle of concert, she tells me that she has boyfriend back in Portugal. That she ask me to concert because she is worried to be girl alone at such a place.'

He sighed deeply. 'And I thought she . . . how do you say?'

'Fancied you?' suggested Tansy.

'Yes.'

'It happens,' sighed Tansy. 'It happens all the time.'

9.30 a.m. On the phone

'Tansy, it's Holly . . . Yes, I know it's early, but this is important . . . No it's not about me and Paul, it's about you and Andy. You have to do something . . . No, it can't wait. I'm coming round.'

10.15 a.m. Sitting on a beanbag in Tansy's bedroom

'Where's Cleo?' Holly asked.

'Her mum's fetching her – she sings in the church choir on Sundays,' explained Tansy. 'Mrs Greenway had a go at my mum, but I told her it was my fault.'

'And what did she say?'

'Oh, a lot of stuff about how Mum should have known better than to give in to a spoilt teenager – spoilt! Me! I wish!'

Tansy flopped down on her bed.

'Anyway,' she said, 'what was it you wanted at such an unearthly hour?'

'You've got to sort this business with Andy,' ordered Holly. 'It simply isn't fair.'

Tansy frowned.

'Why me?'

'He's your boyfriend, for heaven's sake!' exclaimed Holly. 'Or was, till you went all gooey-eyed over José.'

Tansy shook her head.

'Not any more,' she said firmly. 'I do think he is gorgeous, but he's not interested in me. It's his loss.'

She didn't look as if she thought that were completely true, but Holly nodded.

'Right,' she said. 'Now, what about Andy?'

11.30 a.m. 3 Plough Cottages. Testing the waters

'So we thought we would go round to Andy's and tell him straight that his mum isn't dying, she's just pregnant!'

Tansy finished her lengthy explanation to her mother and took another long slurp from her lemonade can.

'No!' Clarity said adamantly. 'You mustn't do that!'

'But, Mrs Meadows,' protested Holly, 'we can't let him go on worrying that his mum has cancer – I mean, I know what I felt like when I thought Dad was going to die.'

Clarity sat down at the kitchen table and pressed her forefingers to her lips.

'Listen,' she said, 'you don't know that Mrs Richards *is* pregnant.'

'But Holly saw her going into the Antenatal place,' said Tansy.

'I know,' said Clarity, 'but it might have been a false alarm. Besides, you two aren't babies any more – if she is expecting a baby, and it's not Doug's child, there will be all sorts of other things to be sorted. It's none of our business.'

'But Mum –'

'No, Tansy,' said Clarity. 'I've just discovered how wrong it is to try to interfere with the way other people choose to do things. I don't recommend it. Just leave it alone. Believe me, there's no other way.'

Ten minutes later
'There is another way, you know,' said Holly, and proceeded to tell Tansy her plan . . .

'That's a great idea!' enthused Tansy. 'When shall we do it?'

'No time like the present,' said Holly. 'Get your coat.'

12.30 p.m. Spilling the beans
Tansy and Holly hovered on Andy's front doorstep.

'Go on then,' urged Holly. 'Do it.'

Tansy pressed the bell.

Within seconds, it was opened by a pretty fair-haired woman.

'Mrs Richards? You don't know us – I'm Tansy and this is –'

'Holly Vine!' exclaimed Andy's mum. 'I remember you from primary school days – you haven't changed a bit.'

'Oh thanks,' muttered Holly.

'And what can I do for you? Andy's out, I'm afraid.'

'Good,' said Tansy. 'In that case, could we come in for a moment, do you think?'

12.45 p.m. Shock tactics

'Now girls,' said Mrs Richards, putting a tray of drinks on the coffee table. 'What can I do for you?'

'Andy thinks you are dying,' said Tansy in a rush.

'He thinks *what*?'

'Oh, we don't,' said Holly. 'We are quite sure you are not dying at all.'

'I'm very relieved to hear it,' said Mrs Richards.

'You're pregnant, aren't you?' said Tansy.

'TANSY!' Holly gasped.

Mrs Richards looked down, coloured, fiddled with a glass and then took a deep breath.

'I don't know how you found out,' she said. 'But you are right. I am expecting.'

Holly gulped.

'Could you tell Andy?' she said. 'Only he thinks you've come home to die.'

To their horror, Mrs Richards clamped a hand to her mouth and let out a strangled sob.

'Oh, poor love,' she said. 'I suppose with me being sick and not eating and . . .'

'And he heard his dad say you had to go to see a doctor before it was too late,' added Tansy. 'Like you were going to die if you didn't go.'

Mrs Richards swallowed hard.

'Thank you for telling me,' she said. 'I'm really very grateful. I'll talk to Andy, but promise me you won't –'

'We never came here,' smiled Holly. 'We've never set foot in the place.'

'Thanks,' said Mrs Richards.

'You *are* going to have it, aren't you?' Tansy asked.

'Tansy!' Even Holly was embarrassed.

'Not it, Tansy. Them. I'm expecting twins. And yes, I'm going to have them.'

1.00 p.m. Owning up

Allegra sat at the dining-room table, pushing a piece of chicken round and round on her plate.

'I can't eat,' she said. 'I feel awful.'

'I don't doubt it,' said her mother. 'Why did you have to do such a thing?'

Jade put down her knife and fork.

'I guess she was so miserable that it seemed the only way to look cool and pretend to be happy,' she said. 'Is that right, Legs?'

Allegra threw her a grateful look.

'Yes,' she admitted. 'I mean, I know it was dumb – but I love Hugo so much and he was eyeing up Candice all the time, and saying that if only I could be more like her, he'd love me even more.'

'And Candice drinks?' queried Paula.

Allegra shrugged.

'They all do,' she said. 'Not that they need to. They're all bubbly and witty and really whacky anyway. I thought if I had a bit of alcohol, I'd be like that as well. And I thought it would help me get the part in *Flying High*.'

'Which you didn't want anyway,' added Jade.

'It would have kept Mum and Dad happy,' sighed Allegra.

Paula leaned across and took Allegra's hand.

'Is that true, Legs?' she asked. 'Are you really fed up with stage school?'

Allegra nodded, her eyes filling with tears.

'I hate it, Mum,' she said softly. 'All I want to do is get out of there. Please let me. Please let me leave.'

'Oh, I do wish your father was here,' cried Paula. 'He'd know what to say.'

'Just say yes, Mum. Please.'

'But what would you do?'

'Go to Jade's school and do A levels,' said Allegra. 'I want to be . . .'

'What?'

'You'll laugh.'

Paula shook her head.

'No, darling, I won't,' she insisted. 'Tell me.'

'I want to be a speech therapist,' she said. 'I don't want to stand on the stage spouting Shakespeare and stuff. I want to help ordinary kids just to talk.'

1.15 p.m. Surprise, surprise!

'Holly, darling, is that you?'

Angela poked her head round the kitchen door

as Holly and Tansy came into the house.

'Yes, sorry I'm late,' called Holly. 'Are we going to the hospital now?'

Angela shook her head.

'I didn't think we'd bother today,' she said.

Holly stared at her.

'Not bother? What do you mean, not bother? We have to go; Dad will be mega upset if we don't. He's worse, isn't he? That's it – he's worse and you're trying to hide it from me. Well, I'm not a kid –'

'Holly!' her mother cried. 'Just go into the sitting room and get my coat then, if you must.'

'So I should jolly well think,' said Holly.

She pushed open the door of the sitting room. There, in an armchair with a rug over his knees, was her dad.

'DAD!' she cried, hurling herself into his arms. 'Oh gosh, sorry. I didn't mean to do that. Have I hurt you? Are you all right?'

Rupert roared with laughter.

'Hang on, laugh carefully,' Holly burst out.

'Holly darling,' he said, 'I'm not going to break. I'm much better. Within a few weeks, I'll be as right as rain.'

Holly did not know whether to laugh or cry.

'Oh, Dad, I'm so pleased you're home,' she said. 'I'll never ever do anything to annoy you ever again. I'm so glad you didn't die.'

Her father smiled.

'Actually,' he said, 'I'm rather chuffed about it too.'

'I'll be a model daughter from now on,' added Holly.

'Oh, please don't,' said her father. 'Then I might expire – from sheer boredom!'

5.30 p.m. Pretending to know nothing

'Hi, Tansy!' Andy was on the doorstep, hopping from one foot to another. 'I've got some amazing news. But you must swear not to tell another living soul. Not yet.'

'Cross my heart and hope to die,' recited Tansy. 'What is it?'

'My mum's not going to die,' he said.

'That's wonderful!' smiled Tansy. 'I'm so pleased.'

'But the thing is,' said Andy, 'she's pregnant.'

'NO!' Tansy tried to look disbelieving. 'Really? I can't believe it!'

'OK, OK, I know she's been away and all,' retorted Andy. 'But it's getting sorted and besides, it's private and no business of anyone's except ours.'

Tansy got the feeling he had learnt that sentence off by heart.

'I'm so happy for you,' she said. 'And I'm sorry I was awful this week. I thought I was being cool and sophisticated and I wasn't. I was being a total jerk.'

Andy grinned.

'You were pretty foul,' he said easily. 'Are we still mates?'

Tansy nodded.

'Of course,' she said.

'Good,' said Andy, his face becoming serious. 'Because I think that over the next few weeks, I might need one.'

8.00 p.m.

Holly was making a start on the three essays she should have written a week earlier when the bell rang.

'Get that, can you, Holly?' her mum called. 'Inspector Morse has just found the body.'

Holly ran to the door to find Tansy clutching a pile of damp washing.

'José left this lot behind,' she said. 'He is back with you, isn't he?'

'Yes,' sighed Holly. 'He's being all enthusiastic and playing Scrabble with my father and puffing up cushions and making tea. It's all very exhausting.'

For a moment, Tansy looked wistful.

'Come on,' said Holly firmly. 'I need you upstairs.'

'What for?' asked Tansy.

'Take your pick,' grinned Holly. 'Biology, French, History . . .'

9.00 p.m. A lesson learned - perhaps?

'Paul's on the phone,' Holly's mother said, bursting into her bedroom. 'He wants to know if you two fancy going over for a game of table tennis.'

'Tell him, thanks but no thanks, not now,' Holly replied.

'You what?' Tansy looked at her in amazement. 'Am I hearing right? Paul wants you and you said no? What on earth for?'

'Because,' said Holly, 'I'm taking my own good advice. I'm playing it cool. Really-laid-back mega cool.'

She waited for thirty seconds.

'Then again, a game of ping-pong is hardly coming on strong, is it?' she said. 'Tansy, get your coat.'